Wild Justice

Books by Priscilla Royal

The Medieval Mysteries
Wine of Violence
Tyrant of the Mind
Sorrow Without End
Justice for the Damned
Forsaken Soul
Chambers of Death
Valley of Dry Bones
A Killing Season
The Sanctity of Hate
Covenant with Hell
Satan's Lullaby
Land of Shadows
The Proud Sinner
Wild Justice

Wild Justice

A Medieval Mystery

Priscilla Royal

Poisoned Pen Press

Poisoned Pen
PRESS

Poisoned Pen Press
4014 N. Goldwater Boulevard, #201
Scottsdale, Arizona 85251
www.poisonedpenpress.com
info@poisonedpenpress.com

Printed in the United States of America

To Diana Smith-Reed, a dear friend,
who introduced me to the works of Sharon Kay Penman.

Acknowledgments

Patrick Hoi Yan Cheung, Christine and Peter Goodhugh, Maddee James, Henie Lentz, Dianne Levy, Paula Mildenhall, Sharon Kay Penman, Barbara Peters (Poisoned Pen Bookstore in Scottsdale, AZ), Robert Rosenwald and all the staff of Poisoned Pen Press, Marianne and Sharon Silva, Lyn and Michael Speakman

"No passion so effectually robs the mind of all its powers of acting and reasoning as fear."

—Edmund Burke,
On the Sublime and Beautiful (1757)

Chapter One

The mist was soft as baby's tears, but the air was as chill as death.

A small party of riders trudged through the muddy ruts and puddles of the well-traveled route. Tall grass and the occasional thick hedge lined the road, now and again encroaching upon it and forcing the armed men to pull their horses closer to the three monastics they protected. As they tried to maintain a respectful distance from the two women, the tall, broad-shouldered monk changed the pace of his horse to make the soldiers' adjustment easier.

Prioress Eleanor shivered, then urged her donkey to a faster gait. Glancing up at Brother Thomas riding just ahead of her, she noticed how the drizzle lay like silver drops on his thick woolen cloak.

Although God might be their ultimate protector, she found an earthly comfort in the strength of this monk. He had been in her service for twelve years, and she knew his gentle nature well, but she could still imagine him leading men into battle like her brother, Baron Hugh of Wynethorpe.

Perhaps it was fortunate, for her peace of mind, that she could not see his face at this particular moment. As he gazed silently into the gloomy haze, his expression was somber for a man who, after many years, had finally learned to smile.

Prioress Eleanor had concerns enough with her talented sub-infirmarian, Sister Anne, who was riding beside her. Although the woman's countenance was hidden, her head covered with a hood against the weather, Eleanor noted with apprehension how thin her friend had grown and how she hunched over her horse, gripping the reins with pale fingers.

I pray she has not fallen ill during this journey, the prioress thought. The ride from Wynethorpe Castle on the border with Wales to Somerset had been cold and arduous.

But Sister Anne had never complained, and her demeanor suggested that even a kind query about her health would be quickly dismissed.

"Fishponds, my lady." Brother Thomas glanced over his shoulder and gestured to the right. "We should arrive soon."

Through the tall but rain-laden grass, she could see them, so large they looked like small lakes that were filled to near-flooding after the deep winter snows had begun to melt. A few weeping willows stood guard along the banks. Their branches, heavy with God's tears, touched the earth. She closed her eyes and offered a silent prayer of thanks that they were finally close to this journey's end.

The road curved sharply around a tall hedge. Through the apple-green grass and behind the drooping boughs of the ancient willows, she could see the dark stone walls of the priory.

"Mynchen Buckland," Thomas said, loud enough for all to hear. "The Hospitallers will greet us with a warm fire and mulled wine to chase away our chill."

Eleanor smiled. Rarely had she felt such relief to arrive at a destination she had never wished to visit.

• • ● • •

Hidden in the thick curtain of the tree branches near the fishponds, a tall man watched the party of travelers disappear through the gates of the women's preceptory. Emblazoned on the left shoulder of his black robe was the eight-pointed white cross of the Hospitallers. His right sleeve, empty below the elbow, flapped awkwardly against his body in the subdued breeze. In his left fist, he grasped a thick walking stick.

Suddenly, he dropped the staff and clutched his mutilated arm to his chest. Whimpering like a colicky babe, he begged God to end the pain that shot like a lightning bolt through the stump where his hand had once been. At least no one could hear his moans and mock him for giving voice to his agony. For that, he was grateful.

As the pain eased, he took a deep breath and sent thanks to God. Indeed, he owed gratitude to Him for other reasons besides the easing of this pain. No longer did he have to dread that someone would reveal how his lower arm had been cut off. They were either dead or otherwise silenced, and that was a profound blessing.

Yet the arrival of these particular monastics at the nuns' house upset his newfound peace. Their reputation for holding up bright candles and bringing light to corners best left dark was well known. If God chose to be kind, the troublesome visitors would accomplish the task that had brought them here and leave after a single night of hospitality and rest. He did not want Prioress Eleanor and her clever monk to linger.

"May You send them back to Tyndal Priory before they find any reason to grow curious," he whispered into the mist.

Another jagged pain struck him, and he knew he must return to his chamber where a numbing draught of poppy syrup and wine awaited him. If he tarried any longer, the pain would become unbearable.

Wincing, he swept up his staff, thrust his stump inside his robe where he could press it against the soothing warmth of his body, and followed the uneven path along the banks of the fishponds. With impatient swipes of his walking stick, he pushed aside the wet grass and offered silent pleas to God.

Only once did he slip in the mud, but he quickly regained his balance and soon vanished into the fog.

● ● ● ● ●

Clumps of black clouds lumbered overhead. The air grew heavier, and large drops of rain began to fall from the slate-colored sky.

Above the din of the rattling downpour, a howling could be heard from an angry squall of wind. It began to lash the tender leaves of trees and pummel the walls that protected the inhabitants of Mynchen Buckland Priory of the Order of the Hospital of Saint John of Jerusalem.

Chapter Two

The small room outside the audience chamber of the Hospitaller prioress was comfortable.

The wait for her to welcome the travelers was not.

Stiffening her back, Eleanor fought to control her temper. Not only had her brother sent timely word to Prioress Amicia that the Prioress of Tyndal would arrive here to present Mynchen Buckland with his gift of rents from the Wynethorpe estates, but she herself had sent a messenger with the specific date of arrival. Her brother's grant, and the knowledge that Baron Hugh had fought in Outremer, should have guaranteed an eager welcome by the woman who ruled this priory in an Order renowned for its hospital at Acre and its brother knights who battled against the infidels.

Her face grew hotter with fury, and she glanced at Brother Thomas.

He paced as if to restore feeling to legs grown stiff after the cold day's long ride. Although he rarely showed impatience, his narrowed eyes suggested he was also less than pleased with the delay.

His own temper must be steaming as much as his robes are, she decided with a short-lived amusement.

Next to her, Sister Anne sat on the bench, a cup of mulled wine clutched in her trembling hands. Despite the crackling fire, the nun shivered in her wet clothing. She tentatively sipped at the wine, and then put the mazer down on a nearby table as if the weight of the cup had become too heavy. Against the pallor of the rest of her face, her cheeks were flushed.

Now truly worried, Prioress Eleanor bent close to whisper an anxious question.

The nun shook her head. "Now that we have this lovely fire, I shall be warmer soon, my lady, and the wine is restorative." As if offering a compromise against further inquiry, she placed her hand around the cup and, with a thin smile, pulled it slightly closer.

The fire snapped and danced. The trio continued to wait, soaked to the bone, hungry, and weary. The door to Prioress Amicia's chambers remained intractably closed, guarded by a grim-faced nun.

A tall, sullen young woman in a plain robe now offered to refill their cups with mulled wine.

With an uncharacteristically sharp tone, Eleanor refused it.

Her eyes ached. At least the soldiers had been sent off to assigned quarters and their horses tended, the prioress thought, but this inexplicable delay in properly welcoming her gift-bearing party of monastics was galling beyond endurance.

Once again, she looked at the black-robed nun who defended the closed door and was uncomfortably reminded of Sister Ruth, her nemesis at Tyndal Priory. How unjust, she thought, looked again, and noted that the only true resemblance between the two was this woman's frown.

A foul temper will accomplish nothing, she decided, and tried to regain some calm. To distract herself, Eleanor turned her attention to their fellow unfortunates who were also waiting for Prioress Amicia to deign to see them.

One man had fallen asleep in a corner near the fire. The heat intensified his sour sweat that mixed with the musty odor coming from his mildewed clothing. His mouth had dropped open, and loud snores punched the air.

Eleanor suspected that his breath was probably foul as well. The few teeth she could see were discolored or dark with rot. That was certainly an uncharitable observation, she said to herself, and sighed. Her attempt to banish her sinful temper had not succeeded as hoped. Unkind thoughts were no less wicked. She turned her attention to the other person in the room. An elderly woman was sitting on a bench near the odiferous man. After the last burst of grating snores, she dragged herself to her feet and, with the aid of a thick piece of wood, hobbled across the room.

Eleanor gestured to her. "Come sit with me at the table, Mistress. It is still warm here but not as..." She discreetly gestured toward the sleeping man and smiled.

Despite having no teeth at all, the aged woman grinned with good humor and eased herself down on the bench. After eyeing her companion up and down, however, her amused expression changed as she realized that the woman with whom she had hoped to amiably gossip was one of significant religious rank.

"I meant no ill, my lady. He's the nuns' steward, a good man to the tenants and always charitable to widows like me. I'm sure he's weary. He's been waiting since early morning to see Prioress Emelyne."

"Prioress Emelyne? I was told Prioress Amicia was the leader here."

"Aye, but not now." The widow looked around and then whispered, "You have not heard what has happened?" Her eyes widened hopefully.

Eleanor shook her head and quickly gestured for the tall maid to bring her companion a cup of wine.

The task was done promptly but with little grace.

Inching closer to the prioress, the widow leaned toward Eleanor's ear. "As I heard the tale, Prioress Amicia was convicted of killing a woman not long ago. While she awaits sentencing by the Hospitaller Prior of England at Clerkenwell, she remains imprisoned here. Prioress Emelyne was chosen by the nuns to take her place until her fate is determined, but no one doubts the new prioress will remain in charge afterward."

Eleanor's first response was disbelief. "What was the source of that tale?"

"It's true enough, my lady! I can assure you of that." Like a mother might with a child, she patted Eleanor's arm to convey confidence in the story's veracity. "From your dress, I see you are not a member of this Order and assume that your priory is not nearby." She smiled, not hiding her curiosity. "I do not recognize your habit, but the wool is fine and does not smell of sheep. I assume you must be of high rank in your own Order?"

"I am from Tyndal Priory near Norwich and belong to the Order of Fontevraud."

With head bowed, the woman sighed. "I know it not, I fear. There are so many Orders these days. It was simpler when most religious were Benedictines or Augustinians with the occasional Cistercian. But I know you all do God's work," she said with a swiftly reverential tone. "And in this wicked world, that is a blessing."

"Please tell me how you learned of this crime."

"Oh, I was about to say! Forgive me for growing distracted. I am so wont to do that now."

"As we all often are," Eleanor replied with gentleness. "Please go on."

"You see, the Hospitaller nuns and lay sisters are freer to move about than I am sure your own nuns are allowed to do."

Eleanor nodded. "Most of our nuns remain sequestered."

The woman's eyes shone with approval. "Not that I am critical, as some are, but the sisters are often in the village and gossip is exchanged. Thus it was with this news."

Unfortunately, the aged widow was unable to say more. The door to the prioress' chamber swung open, and another nun with the white eight-pointed cross on her left shoulder emerged.

Her gaze found Prioress of Tyndal, and she hurried to her.

Eleanor rose and forced a smile.

"If you will, my lady, please come with me. Prioress Emelyne is most eager to greet you."

Chapter Three

Eleanor was not prepared to like this woman who had shown such incivility to weary guests. But when she entered the room, and her wet cloak was taken by the nun who led her there, her first observations urged her to a greater charity.

Prioress Emelyne's chamber was pleasantly warmed by a small fire. Wax candles gave off a flickering but bright glow. As was proper in a priory of this stature, the furniture awaiting visitors and suppliants may have been simple, but it was skillfully crafted. On one wall, there was a window, now shuttered against the damp, but Eleanor suspected it opened onto a bucolic view of the priory as her own did at Tyndal.

Yet it was also clear that the transition from one leader to another had been both sudden and thorny. Accounting rolls were scattered around the floor. Placed closer to the fire, a desk was littered with other parchments, as well as grants and charters with bright waxen seals carefully hung away from the heat. Unlike her own early days at Tyndal, when she needed assistance in taking over from the woman who had preceded her, the Prioress of Tyndal concluded that the Prioress of Mynchen Buckland had been obliged to make sense of her new responsibilities with little help.

Of course, Prioress Emelyne lacked the benefit of an experienced prior to help run her farms, arrange for the collection of rents, and handle other income property. As Eleanor had heard rumored some years ago, the Hospitaller brothers here were often in disagreement with the nuns over the allocation of profits and thus little inclined to cooperation, forcing the resident prioress to be dependent on the snoring steward outside. This was a man whose wages, meat, and ale also came from the brothers next door. To whom did the steward owe his first loyalty?

This is an inefficient arrangement, Eleanor thought. A hired man cared that the earned coin provided him and his family with their needs, not whether the priory was best served. He might well perform his work responsibly, and even out of faith, but a prior considered it part of his sacred duty to God. And should devotion be insufficient motivation, there was the secondary and practical aspect. A prior's efforts determined whether he ate properly and was adequately clothed along with his fellow monastics.

This woman most certainly deserves my gentler sympathy, Eleanor thought.

"Have you been offered wine?" Prioress Emelyne's voice was warm with courtesy.

Eleanor assured her that she had and desired no more.

"I regret the delay in greeting you. Your message arrived, but I fear we expected you later in the day. Yet that is an excuse that offends both the spirit of hospitality and God. I offer my most humble apologies. The nun who brought you to me has orders to make sure your two companions are quickly given food and warm, dry clothes. Your own quarters are being prepared as well, and the monk, who traveled with you, will be taken to the men's house to stay. It is close by."

With an understanding look, Eleanor nodded at the clutter of documents. "I have no wish to delay you further in your duties, but Baron Hugh of Wynethorpe, my brother, gave me specific instructions that the charter granting Mynchen Buckland rents must be given to Prioress Amicia and no other. Neither he nor I were aware that you had replaced her."

Prioress Emelyne's face revealed no hint of her thoughts. "Did he give you an explanation for this very specific edict?"

"Only that he was insistent upon it."

"I fear it is impossible to comply. Perhaps you have not heard…?"

"While I waited outside, I was told that the former prioress, Amicia, has been found guilty of murder and is currently imprisoned here until her sentence is determined in Clerkenwell."

Prioress Emelyne nodded. For a moment, she lowered her eyes suggesting that she was struggling with a response.

Eleanor knew the woman was trying to reply with courtesy but also make it clear that her refusal to obey the baron's command could not be changed. Having no wish to be unreasonable, she reached into her robe, carefully pulled out the document, and handed it over.

"Of course, it is impossible for you to abide by Baron Hugh's demand, but I was obliged to mention it. If you have elder brothers, you know how we must obey them." Briefly, she raised a questioning eyebrow.

"I do." Responding with a cool smile, Emelyne unrolled the charter and began to read.

While she did, Eleanor noted with interest that the woman was not only able to read the Latin with ease but, from her growing expression of amazed pleasure, had swiftly calculated the generosity and how it would enrich her priory. Hugh might not have explained to his sister why he had chosen to honor this priory, but he had told her the immensity of the gift.

"He asks for nothing in return?"

"He is too humble to do so, but he wrote this as he prepared to join King Edward in his current war against the Welsh. I know he would appreciate the prayers of all for his soul." Hugh would ask for no such thing until he lay on his deathbed, as Eleanor well knew, and would scoff should he ever learn of her request, but she chose to ignore his casual faith. If he was going into the Welsh wilderness, she was determined to beg God's protection for him against lethal arrows and unexpected attacks in those dense forests.

"This is most magnanimous. Of course we shall pray for him daily."

"I would also beg a smaller favor."

"Which shall be granted if I am able." Emelyne had hesitated an instant too long.

"I would visit the former prioress, Amicia, in her cell and tell her of my brother's gift. By so doing, I may obey his wishes and truthfully say I did meet with her."

Emelyne appeared about to deny the request.

"Baron Hugh has known her for a long time, and he would be grateful if I did see her, especially because I must send him word of her sad fate." She smiled, hoping to convey her need for this favor to placate a difficult but most generous eldest brother. In truth, Hugh had never mentioned this prioress before, and she had only concluded he must know the woman when he also gave her a private letter to deliver to Prioress Amicia. This particular detail Eleanor had not mentioned to Prioress Emelyne, nor did she intend to do so.

Emelyne's brown eyes darkened into the color of a smoldering coal.

Eleanor's curiosity was sparked. Why this shadow of anger? And why would such a simple entreaty trouble this woman so? Without question, the new prioress was overburdened, but the plea demanded only a simple reply. Were Eleanor refused with a brief but courteous reason, she must accept the decision as surely Emelyne knew.

Emelyne looked again at the charter and rested a finger on the amount of the gift.

"I would prefer the meeting be private," Eleanor said. "Neither you nor I would wish any tales told of this part of my visit." Her supportive tone was calculated to win Emelyne's concurrence.

"An unusual request, but one that may be granted." Emelyne turned to place the charter on the table behind her. Returning her attention to her guest, she said, "There is no danger of violence in a private meeting. Amicia never contested the accusations against her and spends her days praying to God for mercy."

"I will not interrupt her orisons for long. If I could go now, I can honor my brother's wish and leave her in peace."

Emelyne went to the door and gestured to someone outside. "Janeta, her former maid, will take you to the cell," she said to her guest. "Afterward, she will show you to your quarters and make sure you are comfortable. If you wish your evening meal brought to you instead of joining me…"

"If I may, I would prefer to eat in silence with the sisters of the priory so I may contemplate His bountiful mercy as do they."

Emelyne smiled at the hint that her guest did not expect to be entertained at the prioress' table.

And she is also grateful to be relieved of the burden, Eleanor thought, *including my intent to observe silence during the meal.*

When the sullen-faced woman entered, Eleanor saw that she was the one who had previously served the mulled wine. She nodded, and then the two prioresses took courteous leave of each other.

As the Prioress of Tyndal followed the maid to Amicia's cell, she briefly touched the private letter, hidden inside her robes, which Hugh had given her to deliver. At the time, she had asked no questions but assumed that the woman might be the widow of a man whom Hugh had known in Outremer. Many prioresses of high rank were taking vows on the deaths of husbands if they had no wish to remarry. Although Eleanor was curious about this woman, she had not read it, honoring her brother's right to remain silent about both content and reason for writing. At least, she could meet this former prioress who was now condemned as a murderer.

Her eyes on the broad back of the silent Janeta, Eleanor also mused on the inexplicable, albeit short, display of anger exhibited by the prioress. And had there been a growing coolness after the otherwise apologetic and seemingly genuine courtesy with which Prioress Emelyne had initially greeted her and the charitable gift? Perhaps her impression of that had grown out of the long wait they had suffered, as well as her own brittle impatience.

And yet she was certain that something lurked behind the properly phrased courtesy, even if the cause escaped her. Their arrival had been anticipated, so there had been time to plan for the required hospitality. Eleanor had not placed any unexpected or undue burden on the priory when she arrived. Even the usual invitation to dine with the prioress at her table had been politely refused in favor of the simpler meal with the nuns.

Although she could think of no good reason why it would be so, Eleanor could not quite dismiss her budding suspicion that the arrival of their little party at Mynchen Buckland was unwelcome.

Chapter Four

The guard was elderly, bald, and asleep. His patched robe, faded to dull grey, bore a crude Hospitaller cross. As Eleanor and Janeta approached, his eyes flew open. Their brown coloring was so light it almost matched the unbleached white cross. He pressed his fingers against them, trying to clear his vision.

Confused, he nodded at Prioress Eleanor. "Where's Sister Richolda? I don't know this one."

Janeta gestured for him to stand. "Prioress Eleanor of Tyndal Priory. Come to see Sister Amicia."

Clumsily pulling himself onto his feet, he jerked his head up and down with awkward courtesy. "She's a murderer, my lady. Quiet, though. Prays, mostly."

"I am to have an audience with her, alone, and with the door shut." Eleanor kept her tone gentle, although firm enough to prevent any argument. Some might call the man's behavior boorish, but she felt no ill will in him, and therefore took no offense.

"And safe enough to visit alone," he replied, now rubbing a hand against his bristled cheek. "God knows there is no need to even guard her. We could leave the door open, and she wouldn't try to escape. Very docile for a murderer." He blinked at the prioress as if surprised to discover he was speaking to someone other than himself. "Not that I have known other killers. Maybe..." He hesitated, trying to find more words to express whatever it was he had intended to say.

Janeta cleared her throat and gestured at the door.

Truly a woman of few words, the prioress thought.

The guard banged on the cell door with the palm of his hand and then pressed his ear to the wood.

"Just to let her know in case she's on the pot or asleep," he muttered before inserting a key to unlock the door.

As the door opened, he immediately stepped back, but Janeta headed toward the open door.

"I wish to be alone with Sister Amicia," Eleanor said. She thought she had been quite clear about this. Perhaps Janeta had served Amicia so long that she was accustomed to remaining by her side even during private conversations? Yet she was young and thus unlikely to have been a treasured servant of many years. Might the woman lack wits? That had not been apparent. Eleanor simply didn't know.

Janeta stood aside and bowed her head. Her reaction was unreadable.

Eleanor went inside and firmly shut the door. She noticed that no one locked it behind her.

● ● ● ● ●

The dimly lit room smelled dry and clean. Against the stone wall, Eleanor could see a bed, presumably with a straw mattress, a tiny chest, a table, and a bench to sit on for meals. On the table, a candle flickered in a simple holder, a needed source of light because there was no window in the room.

As her eyes adjusted to the shadows, she concluded that the place was austere but not uncomfortable. It was slightly bigger but otherwise little different from quarters familiar to most nuns in a larger priory.

The former Prioress Amicia was kneeling in front of a roughly formed cross hanging on the wall. If she prayed, it was silently. But the delay in greeting her visitor was brief. She stood, folded her hands into her sleeves, and turned to face Eleanor with all the dignity of an older woman who still held high ecclesiastical rank.

"I am Eleanor, Prioress of Tyndal Priory and sister of Baron Hugh of Wynethorpe."

It was hard to tell in the muted light, but Amicia's expression seemed not to change, although her eyes might have briefly widened. "You are most welcome," she replied. "My dead husband also went to Outremer to fight. Before he left, your brother brought him advice on the many details of such a pilgrimage and visited our castle to offer instructive tales he had learned from others who had returned from there."

"Your husband was martyred in the cause?" At least, she had been right about the reason for Hugh's acquaintance with this former prioress.

"He died in an accident not long after his return." The woman announced this with no hint of sorrow.

In courtesy, Eleanor bowed her head to express the requisite sympathy.

"I fear I have no sustenance or wine to offer you." Amicia gestured at the bare room. "I assume that Prioress Emelyne provided both on your arrival."

"She did." A small lie, but Eleanor saw no need to say otherwise. Quickly retrieving her brother's hidden letter, she handed it to Amicia. "Baron Hugh sent me with a charter of rents as a gift to this priory and this personal letter to you. Both were supposed to be given to you only…"

"I assume the charter has been presented to Prioress Emelyne. As I well understand, that part of his wish could not be obeyed." Amicia took the letter in one hand, briefly pressing it close to her breast before dropping the hand to her side.

Eleanor told her the terms of her brother's gift. "Prioress Emelyne knows nothing of this letter, however, nor do I know the contents. I felt I must honor his precise wishes in this one respect."

"That decision was extremely kind, Prioress Eleanor. I am sure you know that I have been accused of murder, found guilty by all in Chapter, and now await the final verdict on punishment by our prior in Clerkenwell."

"God is your judge, not I, and…"

The former prioress held up a hand. "There is no need to say more. I have not contested the judgment."

Eleanor nodded and fell silent.

Amicia opened the letter, bent closer to the candle, and began to read.

Watching the woman, Eleanor concluded that, for whatever reason the former prioress had committed the crime, she had been suffering for her deed. Despite the subdued light, she could see the slack flesh on Amicia's face and neck, suggesting she had lost weight. There was a jagged scar that sliced through her upper lip, although that may have been an old wound. Her wrists looked like fragile twigs, yet her hands were swollen. As Amicia turned to read another part of the letter, Eleanor noted the woman's eyes. Sunken deep into her skull, they reflected the glittering flame of the candlelight like pools of black water.

It was an eerie sight, and she shivered. Quickly, she turned her thoughts elsewhere.

Of all the Orders he might have chosen to grant such generous rents, why did her brother choose the Hospitallers? Eleanor knew so little of Hugh's life in Outremer. Was it because his friend's widow had joined the Order, or was there another reason? She knew he had been wounded at least once. Perhaps he had been healed by the Hospitallers in Acre?

Although she should chastise herself for it, Eleanor realized she also longed to know more about this crime and the person who had committed it. Here was a woman whose name she had never heard, yet her brother had taken the time to write her a letter, something he rarely did even to his own sister.

Of course I am curious, Eleanor said to herself. It is no sin to want to understand what pain my brother must have suffered on crusade, or even to want to understand why he had granted this gift. Although he was the head of the family and had every right to make such decisions without consulting her or explaining his intent, he often did both. Despite the difference in their ages and long separation, they had developed a deeper bond since their father's death.

Suddenly, Amicia looked up at her visitor and sucked in her lips as if struggling to control an emotion too overwhelming to endure. With a cry, she sank to the floor, letter still clutched in her hand, and began to weep.

Dropping to her knees, Eleanor put a hand on the woman's bony shoulder. "Let me summon help! If you do not have an infirmarian..."

Amicia grasped her arm, looking up at Eleanor with an expression of agony. "I do not need Sister Richolda. It is your help I beg."

"What can I offer...?"

"I know your reputation well, my lady. Please, in the name of our merciful God, prove me innocent of this murder. I swear to you, on any hope I may still have of Heaven, that I never committed the foul deed for which I have been condemned!"

And with that she thrust herself into Eleanor's arms and sobbed uncontrollably.

Chapter Five

Eleanor was profoundly shaken by what had just occurred. Quietly shutting the door to the cell, she took a deep breath to recover her calm and then turned to Janeta and the guard.

Neither seemed to notice her distress.

"Does she want for anything?" Janeta gestured at the closed door with evident uneasiness.

The maid may be abrupt and sullen in manner, Eleanor thought, but she shows great concern for her former mistress. Perhaps she belonged to the few who believed her innocent, or else she was one of those servants so loyal the verdict did not matter.

"Only to be left in peace," the prioress replied in a kind voice.

In truth, Amicia had told Eleanor that she found increasing solace in the quiet of her murky cell. At her request, meals were delivered and removed without a word by the server. Prioress Emelyne had ceased to come, and the priest visited only when Amicia called for him. She tolerated the obligatory visits by the infirmarian, but those would end soon. The ailment she was treating, the former prioress said, would not trouble her for long.

"She's never a bother," the guard said, jabbing a finger into his mouth as if a tooth hurt. Then his eyes widened, and he hurried to lock the door as if just remembering that it confined a murderer inside.

"Shall I take you to your quarters, my lady?" The brief light in Janeta's eyes had faded, and once again her gaze was as dull as her tone.

"I wish to see Sister Anne and Brother Thomas first. Please take me to them."

Janeta brusquely nodded and strode off like a lady of rank who fully expected her minions to follow close behind.

Deep in thought, Eleanor trailed the maid along the stone corridor. As the distance from the cell increased, her uneasiness over Amicia's plea and the decision to help her grew greater.

Might she have been bewitched by the darkness in the cell and only now, in the brightness of God's light, able to see how the Devil had weakened her reason and used her for some evil purpose? Was Amicia a killer, after all?

She forgot Janeta and paused by a window to watch the sunlight dance and play with the raindrops on a nearby roof.

When the former prioress had suddenly begged help to prove her innocence, Eleanor was shocked. So why had she agreed to the appeal?

I am not inexperienced in the devious ways of mortals, she thought. Those who initially confess to a crime often claim later to be guiltless. Amicia might not face a hanging, but the Prior of England would not otherwise grant her much mercy. To be stripped of her habit and sent out into the world, with little more than a thin patched robe to hide her nakedness, was not a kind fate.

Whatever her worldly rank, let alone the religious one, Eleanor knew that few friends or family would grant sanctuary to a convicted murderer and especially a prioress cast out by her Order. Nevertheless, whether God or Satan had inspired this decision to help the woman, Eleanor had given her word. She and her companions would do what they could to find the truth. If God willed it, they would succeed.

As she again mulled over the tale told by the former prioress, and especially her demeanor as she told it, she was still convinced by Amicia's story. The difficulty in proving it remained immense. As she had told the weeping woman, there was little hope they would find proof good enough to change the conviction. The corpse had been buried. The location of the murder had been sullied. No evidence likely remained.

What she did not say to Amicia, but surely the woman must know, was that the Fontevraudine monastics were also strangers here with no authority beyond common courtesy. In the unlikely event that they could question all witnesses and the residents of the nuns' preceptory or the brothers' nearby house, which ones could they trust to tell the truth? They knew no one. And asking the former prioress for the names of the honest was deliberately tilting the scales of justice.

Eleanor felt as if she and her two religious were floating in a sea mist, only this one was made of ignorance. All she could give was her word to try, but that alone seemed to have given ease to Amicia.

From the corner of her eye, she saw something move. Startled out of her musing, she turned.

Janeta waited nearby, her silence heavy with impatience.

"Did you serve Sister Amicia for many years?" The question was an awkward one, but Eleanor had to start somewhere.

"I serve her still." Janeta turned around and began to walk away again without turning her head.

Feeling a bit like a duckling trailing a hen, Eleanor dutifully followed. "You are allowed into her cell to wait on her?"

Amicia had not mentioned any visits from her maid, although she had spoken of the priest and even those who served her meals. Was Janeta's presence of less significance to her than a mazer or trencher? Yet the maid's devotion suggested a closer bond, and she most certainly would gain nothing by maintaining such loyalty to a religious convicted of murder.

"I accompany Sister Richolda each week when she comes to treat my mistress. She is the infirmarian here."

Desperate to glean any information, Eleanor asked another question. "Will you stay and join the Order as a lay sister, if your mistress is cast forth from the priory, or follow her?"

Janeta spun around, her face red. "My future shall be determined by God's will, my lady. I pray each day for His guidance." Then she resumed striding down the corridor.

"As we all must do, my child." Eleanor called after. Tired of patiently chasing after the maid, she stopped and felt her face grow hot with fury at the rank discourtesy shown her.

Yet despite the rudeness, the prioress knew her anger should be directed at herself, not Janeta. Eleanor's questions had been ill-phrased and badly considered. If she were to investigate this crime, in a place where she did not know friend from foe, she must be both cautious and wise in her methods.

The logical thing was to tell Prioress Emelyne that the former prioress now wanted to claim she was innocent, but Amicia had forbidden it. All available evidence had been considered in the Chapter meeting of nuns who found enough to condemn, she said, and she respected their fair judgment. She knew of nothing new and significant to change their minds. To demand a reopening of the decision based on what they had already considered would be a profound insult.

Eleanor did ask why the former prioress had refused to defend herself.

In reply, Amicia asked her if she would reverse her own judgment, having found someone guilty on adequate testimony, solely because the convicted criminal now pled innocence but could offer nothing of significance to explain why.

Noting the patent evasion, Eleanor chose to concede the woman's point and not pursue her query.

Halfway down the hall, Janeta again waited, hands clutched to her waist.

The Prioress of Tyndal ignored her.

After a brief hesitation, the maid retraced her steps. Her expression was now humble as she dutifully lingered until the prioress gave her a command.

Eleanor, however, was lost in thought.

The first problem, she decided, was to find a way to remain here longer than she had planned. Normally, they would have accepted the priory's charitable hospitality for a night or two at most, depending on the weather. Considering the difficulties involved in this kind of investigation, they might well need several days, but she knew they did not dare stay much longer. Again she reminded herself that, although she had sworn to Amicia that she would make an honest attempt to reverse the conviction, she had also made it very clear there was little hope.

Without question, she knew Brother Thomas would be eager to help. As for Sister Anne, Eleanor had doubts. After the deaths of the abbots last winter, when the sub-infirmarian struggled to find the causes for their deaths and illnesses, she had suffered from melancholy. Never plump, she had become skeletal. Eleanor questioned the wisdom of engaging her in another murder investigation so soon after that last one, but she would let her friend decide what she wanted to do.

The prioress turned to Janeta and nodded, indicating she was now ready for the maid to resume leading her to where her companions were waiting.

Meanwhile, I must come up with a reasonable excuse to linger here that does not betray my true intent, Eleanor thought. If we find no indisputable evidence to prove the Chapter verdict in error, Prioress Emelyne will suffer no insult. If we do, I will decide the best way to present it then.

As Janeta approached the dining hall where the two monastics were presumably eating a warm meal, the maid stumbled slightly on the uneven stone floor.

Eleanor had her answer. Without further hesitation, she flung herself to the ground and cried out.

Janeta spun around and reacted with horror as she saw the Prioress of Tyndal writhing on the stone floor in agony.

"My ankle!" Eleanor grabbed her foot and hunched over it grimacing with severe pain. "Summon Sister Anne and Brother Thomas to me immediately! I fear I have broken it. I need their help."

With praiseworthy speed, Janeta ran to the hall to bring them.

Chapter Six

Sister Anne knelt by her friend's side. "Where is your injury?"

Brother Thomas, his brow furrowed with worry, stood a short distance away.

Standing over the prioress, a fist pressed against her mouth, Janeta whimpered. Her wide-eyed look did not clarify whether she grieved more out of sympathy for the injury or fear of reprisal because her negligence had allowed it to occur.

Catching Thomas' attention, Eleanor subtly indicated that she wished him to lead the maid further away.

The monk immediately turned to Janeta and took her to a more private place down the hall where he began offering consolation.

As she pointed to her ankle, Eleanor loudly proclaimed, "I think it is broken!" Then she gestured for Anne to bend closer. "Decide it is badly sprained," she whispered. "I deliberately fell and am quite well."

Anne felt the ankle.

Eleanor cried out in pain.

Trying not to smile at the prioress' realistic performance, the sub-infirmarian decided to thoroughly examine the ankle anyway, despite her friend's protestations. It was sound.

"I feel no broken bone, my lady," the sub-infirmarian announced with fitting gravity, "but you have probably suffered a serious injury." She looked around. "I would prefer to examine your foot more thoroughly, but your modesty would be offended if I did so in this public place."

"Then I must be carried to my chambers. I cannot stand by myself."

Anne rose and called out to Janeta. "We must assist the Prioress of Tyndal to her quarters." She gestured for the maid to stand by her stricken leader. "Wait here while I confer with Brother Thomas."

The maid did as commanded. Whatever the monk had said seemed to have done little to calm her trembling.

Anne stood as close as she dared to the monk and whispered, "She is well but has some cause for feigning injury. As soon as I have spoken with her in private, I shall send word to you."

Although he bowed his head quickly, he did not do so fast enough to hide from her the sparkling amusement in his eyes. "I will be lodged with the brothers in the house nearby," he said with proper solemnity. "The priory steward is to take me there. As soon as I hear from you, I shall return to offer our prioress God's comfort."

Giving him a quick wink, Anne watched him return to the dining hall and then went to her prioress' side. With ease, she and Janeta lifted the tiny prioress, braced her between them, and transported her to the chambers which she and the sub-infirmarian were to share.

• • ● • •

Once settled on the edge of her bed, Prioress Eleanor submitted with firmly gritted teeth to a more thorough examination of her ankle.

"You were fortunate not to break it, my lady, but I fear you will not be able to stand or ride for several days, perhaps longer. To do so, might cause the bone to shatter."

Nodding with sadness, Eleanor turned to the maid and first praised Janeta for the gentle strength with which she had helped Sister Anne carry her. "You bear no responsibility in this accident, my child," she said. "I was clumsy and did not see the uneven stone. Should anyone fault you, they may come to me. I shall declare you free of any blame."

Color began to return to the maid's pale face.

"But you must immediately bear a message for me to Prioress Emelyne. Although I had hoped to leave here at daybreak after a night's rest, I fear we are obliged to now beg the Mynchen Buckland Priory for the kindness of a longer hospitality. I would speak to your gracious prioress about this as soon as possible."

With an abrupt bow of her head, Janeta fled to obey the request.

• • ● • •

As she shut the door behind the departing maid, Anne turned with a bemused look to her prioress. "Why have you done this?"

"Because the former prioress, now Sister Amicia, has begged us to prove her innocent of murder."

"And you believed this new tale? I overheard what the old woman told you before you were admitted to the prioress' chambers." Anne put a gentle hand on her friend's arm. "Please do not think I question your decision, but I confess amazement."

Eleanor rose from the bed and went to pour some wine that had been left by the priory servants as refreshment for them both.

"I, too, was stunned by this change of plea, but I found her tale oddly credible. Sister Amicia confirmed that she was accused of murdering a widow named Mistress Hursel in the cloister garth after she was discovered with blood staining her hands and bending over the dead woman. At no time did she deny the accusation, although she also did not confess to the crime."

"Not to confess or deny? The tale grows stranger." Anne frowned. "But let me ask if you know why anyone thought she would have done this vile thing?"

"When the trial began in Chapter, no one gave a reason why, but she admitted to me that she had known Mistress Hursel before she had taken vows. The dead woman had been in her service."

"No grounds were given for the crime? That alone should have led many to question the accusation. The logical assumption would have been that the prioress had simply found the body, and someone else was guilty of the murder."

Eleanor sipped her wine with pleasant surprise. If the priory was not pleased with their visit, they did not show their displeasure in the quality of wine they served. Then she said to Sister Anne, "Here the tale grows more complicated. Sister Amicia told me that because some here knew that she and the murdered woman were known to each other, she admitted at the trial that she had not only known the dead woman but that they had quarreled soon after her own husband's death. It was over a minor issue, she said, but heated enough that she released Mistress Hursel from her service."

"Had I been in Chapter, I would have wanted to know more about the quarrel. That confession does not argue well for innocence, yet it does not condemn her. She voluntarily spoke of it. Were she guilty, she would not have been so inclined."

"I do not think anyone asked for more details during the trial, but I did. She would only repeat that Mistress Hursel had once been in her service, offended her, and she had then let her go. But she also claimed she had set the quarrel aside long ago, forgiven her, and thus had no cause to kill her. All sins she had committed before she took vows were confessed to a priest, after which she performed the penance required. Since that time, she has tried to banish any ill will from her heart and concentrate on God's forgiving love." Eleanor put down her cup. "Those were Sister Amicia's words, not mine."

Anne shook her head. "Why even tell the story of the quarrel and why refuse to defend herself at the Chapter trial?"

"The answer to your first question was that she did not wish to hide her sin of anger against Mistress Hursel."

"An ill-advised statement to make in a murder trial, but I respect her candor."

"The answer to your second is far less credible. She refused to give me any details when I asked. Her only response was to say her purpose was irrelevant and would not make any difference in reopening the verdict."

"That explanation is absolutely implausible. If she were innocent, I can think of no reason not to say so at the time. Yes, I have known some who were so shaken by an event that they could not speak or act with sense for a while, but her senses should have returned in time to deny guilt at the trial." She shook her head. "The evidence against her was weak, yet her own behavior screams of guilt."

"You are right. The nuns might have come to a different verdict if she had denied guilt and made any effort to defend herself, but she utterly refused to do so. I fear that, plus her willingness to admit to a quarrel with Mistress Hursel, led to the verdict." Eleanor picked up her cup and stared into it as if seeking solutions. "If we set her strange behavior aside, however, the verdict troubles me too. Is there more to her condemnation than she knew or has she failed to tell me something? Neither, can I answer."

Anne finished her wine and rubbed the mazer between her hands as she thought. "Why change her mind and now beg to be proven innocent?"

"Her decision came after hearing of my brother's gift and reading his letter."

Anne raised an eyebrow in question. She didn't need to explain. They both knew Hugh's fondness for bedding married women.

Eleanor shook her head. "I think not, or at least nothing in what she said suggested they had been lovers. She mentioned briefly that my brother and her husband had been friends, both going on pilgrimage to fight in Outremer, albeit at different times. After she became a widow, Hugh showed her great kindness and supported her when she chose to take vows. An old and loyal friendship with the dead spouse might well explain why he wrote to her and the reason for the gift."

"So your brother revealed only a fondness based in his friendship with the husband?" Anne was not absolutely convinced.

"My brother is the definition of the virtue of discretion. He has never mentioned her, and I have learned of some of his favored women." She smiled. "I have also learned to look beyond his words and even count the number of times he blinks when he speaks of certain women."

The sub-infirmarian laughed. "Then what could have been in the letter that made her change her mind?"

"She said that, although his generous gift had profoundly moved her, the mention of the Wynethorpe family reminded her that he had a sister with some reputation in the search for justice. When she realized that the sister now stood before her, she felt hope that we three could help her."

"I must go back to the question of why she allowed herself to be condemned for an atrocity she did not commit. She gives no details to explain why, although the reason must be more important than she now maintains. For some time, she has had occasion to face her likely expulsion from the Order and resultant severe hardship in the world, yet she has remained silent and accepted her fate. Now, quite suddenly, she talks of hope?"

"She offered only one excuse for changing her plea. After her trial, she began to comprehend that she had erred in accepting guilt. It was a sin. I find this sudden realization as questionable as you clearly do."

Anne drank her wine in silence, and then gestured to the ewer.

Eleanor nodded, and the sub-infirmarian poured more for them both.

"There is much I should have liked to question her about, but I did not have the time to do so," the prioress said. "Perhaps she accepted guilt to protect someone else? If so, has that person since escaped so any revelation of her own innocence no longer offers a threat to the guilty one?" She raised her hands in question. "Although she will not hang for the murder, she will not survive long in the world once she is cast forth. Because of that, I even wondered if this was the means for her to commit self-murder, but I think it unlikely. Her demeanor overall suggested a sad resignation but, her brief tears aside, not profound melancholy.

"Why did you believe her?"

"She looked relieved to admit innocence, as one is when finally confessing a lie."

"What a perplexing woman. First she claims to repent of telling what she now insists is a lie, and yet we both think her current tale holds falsehoods too. If that is true, what sin has she cast aside?"

Eleanor concurred. "Those who must face hanging often claim innocence even when they have actually confessed to their crime. They weep as well, but those tears are based in terror of the execution. But her tears seemed genuine. As you said, this woman has lived with her fate and never shrunk from it until today." She bit her lips. "I know my belief in her story is not based in logic, and yet..."

"Did she give any further details about what happened that day?"

"A few. Her maid, Janeta, announced Mistress Hursel's arrival, stating that the woman awaited her in the cloister garth. When Amicia approached, she saw the woman sitting on a bench, head forward as if asleep. She put a hand on her shoulder to gently awaken her, but Mistress Hursel fell forward. Fearing the woman was ill, she grabbed her to prevent injury. That was how Amicia got blood on her hands. Although she did not see the cause of the wound, she knew the woman was dead and was about to raise the hue and cry, but the Hospitaller priest, Father Pasche, arrived. The moment he caught sight of her, he fell to his knees and asked, "Prioress Amicia, what have you done?""

Anne clapped her hands in frustration. "All she needed to do was tell the truth!"

"I did wonder aloud why the priest assumed she had done something wrong. In response, she said that he had cause. He knew of the quarrel between herself and the dead woman."

"Was she the first to speak of it at the trial or was he?"

"It was she."

Putting her empty cup back on the chest next to the ewer, Anne frowned. "It is as if she wanted to be found guilty."

"I agree. Yet now she does not. If she had cause for lying about her guilt before, something has since happened to change her mind or, perhaps, the reasons for her doing so have altered. I am not convinced my brother's generous gift and the reminder that we have solved a few crimes were why she changed her mind, any more than I believe her sudden realization that lying is a sin. She has been a prioress and fully aware that she must tell the truth in confession. Sin may creep up on us, but, soon after, we know the nature of our transgression." Eleanor took a deep breath. "All that noted, my heart still found her innocence believable."

"Your heart is rarely wrong."

"I promised her nothing more than an attempt. Finding evidence at this point is virtually hopeless. Yet strangers rarely invade a priory, kill, and then disappear without a trace. The most likely conclusion is that someone here, or very familiar to the monastics, killed Mistress Hursel. In any case, that is the premise with which we must start."

"And your contrived injury will allow a few days for investigation."

"Sister Amicia has refused to let me tell Prioress Emelyne of her changed story unless we find new evidence. Hard as that is to accept, I had to agree and feel some sympathy for her decision. Clearly, all inquires must be cautiously subtle. I have eliminated myself from seeking answers because of my injury, but Brother Thomas is free to do what he can at the men's house and that includes questioning the priest. You must go to him and relay what I have told you. As my counselor, he may always confer with me in private without raising suspicion."

Sister Anne waited for her friend to continue. When she did not, she reached out to touch Eleanor's arm. "Request of me whatever you need. I have the freedom of the nun's priory and also have access to you as your sub-infirmarian."

"I would not ask more of you than you are able."

Sister Anne waved that hesitation aside. "I need a task. I am not accustomed to remaining idle when there is work to be done."

Eleanor took her friend in her arms and hugged her. Their friendship was deep enough that nothing more need be said.

There was a hesitant knock at the door.

Eleanor quickly lay back on the mound of pillows.

When Sister Anne opened the door, Janeta stood outside, a tray of food in her hands.

Chapter Seven

Prioress Emelyne was in a rage.

To keep from ramming her fist into the stone wall as she strode back to her quarters after speaking with Prioress Eleanor, she struck her thigh hard but felt no pain.

Desperately, she prayed for composure. Expected to be the model of devotion for her nuns, Emelyne knew she was obliged to remain tranquil even when outrage coursed like hellfire through her veins.

Why had God cursed her with these wearisome guests?

Not that she suspected they had intentionally created a reason for a longer stay. They had no motive to do so, and the stone floor was uneven. Last winter, an elderly nun had fallen, broken her hip, and subsequently died. Although Prioress Eleanor was much younger and seemingly did not suffer from poor vision, her fall might well have been due to prayerful distraction. Emelyne had heard that many considered this leader of Tyndal Priory a woman much favored by God. Hadn't He granted her a vision of the Holy Family some years ago?

She shivered as a damp breeze whistled through a window in the corridor and struck her overheated cheeks with a sharp chill. Looking outside, she saw that the sun was bravely attempting to shine through the mist. That might be a blessing, but it did nothing to calm her anger born of an uneasy spirit and a fear she could not quite define.

An approaching nun murmured a greeting and bowed her head with reverence.

Prioress Emelyne brushed past in grim silence.

As she approached her chambers, the nun standing without opened the door so her leader could enter.

Emelyne barked an order for mulled wine.

The nun swiftly obeyed.

At least the fire is cheerful, the prioress thought, and threw herself into the chair. The floor remained cluttered with accounting rolls and charters. Only the gift from Baron Hugh rested alone in the middle of her desk.

"A blessing and a curse," the prioress muttered, her words punctuated by the snapping flames. "Had he not chosen to be generous, his sister would not have arrived with her companions to disturb my peace."

Yet the gift was welcome. She could now afford to improve the fishponds, which had grown rank with foul growth, and the surrounding paths, which dissolved into treacherous mud in the rain. Had the meeting with her steward not been interrupted by the news that Prioress Eleanor had been injured and required her attendance, she might have discussed other priorities that could be funded, thanks to the baron's munificence.

There was a soft knock at the door

Emelyne granted leave to enter, and the nun hurried to place the requested hot wine next to her leader's hand.

"Stay outside, Sister. I wish to be left alone," Emelyne said and waved the woman away.

A sip of the wine soothed her, and her thoughts, previously scattered by her anger, began to coalesce.

Until she proved to the Prior of England that she was a talented manager of priority assets, she did not want him to learn of her outbursts of unseemly wrath. In spite of her acknowledged competence, she knew that the nuns had voted for her to replace Prioress Amicia with some reluctance. Many were aware of her occasional failure to curb her hot temper.

But the Prior would forgive a few complaints about excessive beatings or harsh fasts if she succeeded in increasing this priory's expected donations to the Hospitaller work in Outremer. God's demands were paramount. The funding of charity work and brother knights would take precedence over the grumblings of feeble women whose flesh longed for earthly comforts and thus resented a holier austerity.

She sighed, drank a little deeper of the wine, and felt her ire recede a bit more.

If only these Fontevraudine religious would leave and let her proceed with her work of getting the priory assets in order. But that wish must be set aside. She could not change either the fact of the visit or the accident that would keep them here.

Staring at the ceiling, she considered her plight and her options.

What danger was there in this extended visit by Prioress Eleanor and her companions? As Baron Hugh's sister, she knew about the long friendship he had had with the former Prioress Amicia and her dead husband. Had there been time enough for the news of her murder conviction to have reached him? Might he have asked his sister and Brother Thomas to look into the matter?

Despite her orders, there was a soft knock at the door.

Squeezing her eyes shut to control her surging fury, Prioress Emelyne bade the nun enter.

The woman bowed her head. "I beg forgiveness, my lady, but your steward has asked if he may be permitted to return to his other duties after he takes the Fontevraudine monk to his quarters."

"Tell him he must come back here," she replied, then forced a smile. "I have many other pressing matters to discuss."

As soon as the nun closed the door, Emelyne picked up the cup of mulled wine and drained it. Peaceful warmth now rapidly seeped through her, and she sat back in her chair with greater content. *Surely there is no reason to be troubled,* she decided, *and my fear is only a woman's frailty.*

The news of the murder could not have traveled yet to Wyne-thorpe Castle. Even if it had, the baron would have learned as well that Amicia consented to her verdict without offering one word of denial or argument in her own defense. Why then would Baron Hugh question the verdict and ask his sister to intervene? Emelyne caught herself smiling benignly at the winking flames of her little fire. After all, she mused, Prioress Eleanor was unable to walk on that wounded ankle. What trouble could she possibly cause, even if her brother had hoped she would look into the verdict as a kindness to the widow of a fellow crusader?

There was Brother Thomas to consider, but he would be quartered in the brothers' house. All she had to do was ask Brother Damian to set a watch on the clever monk and make sure he did nothing to investigate this murder or communicate with his prioress.

About Sister Anne, she had few worries. The nun's expertise lay in healing and the nature of injuries. There was no corpse for her to examine or anything else that might require her medical expertise. Although Mynchen Buckland's own infirmarian, Sister Richolda, could be sent to attend Prioress Eleanor, Tyndal's leader would surely prefer her own healer to provide any needed physic.

And, having noted the sub-infirmarian's gauntness and pallor, Emelyne wondered if the nun was in frail health. If that observation was correct, then caring for her prioress would be all Sister Anne was capable of doing.

"God has given me wisdom in my time of trial," the Prioress of Mynchen Buckland murmured and then sighed with growing confidence. "I take it as a sign that my elevation to this position finds favor in His eyes, and that my willingness to endure penance for my sins has been accepted."

She waited. There was only silence, which led her to conclude she had been right about God's smile upon her. To further support this belief, she was suddenly graced with a new inspiration.

Wouldn't Janeta be the perfect one to report any attempts by Prioress Eleanor to pry into the murder of Mistress Hursel or to contact Brother Thomas for assistance on her behalf?

The secular maid would soon be without a mistress, once the Prior of England cast Amicia from the Order. With no means of support, Janeta would be desperate to gain favor with the new prioress who had the authority to accept her as a lay sister, should she be willing to take vows. If Janeta were assigned to wait upon Prioress Eleanor, until the woman was well enough to leave, the maid dare not refuse Emelyne's command to bring her all pertinent news.

In a voice some might deem too merry for a prioress, Emelyne called to the nun waiting outside her door and told her to bring Janeta to her chambers before the steward arrived.

Chapter Eight

Little rivulets ran along the short path between the nuns' preceptory and the brothers' house. Usually the route was dry, but the severe winter and unusual snows had turned this part of Somerset into more than the usual wetlands. Men sank up to their ankles in muck. Oxen bellowed in fear when they stumbled. Placid streams now raged, churning with tan mud and torn black roots. Deep puddles formed in the ruts dug by cart wheels.

Brother Thomas wondered if the very walls of Mynchen Buckland Priory might be in danger of cracking. Turning around, he quickly decided that the buildings were on high enough ground. As the mud sucked hungrily at his feet, he concluded that only the path was a problem.

"There is no danger to either the preceptory or the brothers' house," the odiferous steward said as he noted the expression on the monk's face. "But even the water in the fishponds has risen to flood stage and grown filthy with earth crumbling from the banks. If a man fell in, there are a few places he might be entangled by the rank weeds and drown. We are sure-of-foot here, and there is little real danger of that." He grinned impishly. "Now a stranger would be well-advised to try netting his fish elsewhere."

Thomas smiled. The man might reek, but he was otherwise a pleasant fellow. Perhaps in summer, when his clothes could dry and not mildewed, he would be less fragrant. "We passed the ponds on our journey here," he said. "I have never seen ones so large. Is there not an island, or even two?"

"Aye, but nothing lives there. And we are fortunate the ponds are so large. The fish will likely survive the flooding and mud."

"Do the brother knights and sergeants pay for the maintenance?"

"There is only one knight, Brother, and no sergeants." He gestured at the building they approached. "But I think the nuns will quickly agree to pay for repairs, now that Prioress Emelyne leads the nuns' preceptory. The two houses should be on better terms."

"There was a quarrel?" Thomas already knew about the tension between the two houses here and that it was firmly based in disparate income. The women vastly outnumbered the men and had title to more of the rents and lands donated to the Order, but the men often felt aggrieved over their lesser financial standing and let their feelings be known. Thus his question was intended to uncover something more. Friction often revealed much about the character of the arguing parties. With a murder to investigate, such information could be helpful.

The steward shrugged. "In my opinion, 'twas a trivial thing. No one went hungry or badly clothed. Prioress Amicia, as she once was, dealt fairly with the men, fierce though she was in defense of the nuns' rights to the gifts they were given. The men have to pay for the maintenance, ritual garments, and other costs of the priest, a man both houses share to keep their souls clean." He beamed, exposing irritated gums and darkened teeth. "And they provide me with two meals a day, but I also require a good sum for my skills. The men pay that as well. Although the nuns have far more work for me, the men resent that I spend most of my time working for the preceptory."

Thomas raised a questioning eyebrow, although his expression betrayed no criticism.

"I have a wife and children, Brother. I care not who gives me my pennies, but Roger de Veer, the Prior of England in the last king's reign, decided that the brothers would pay the steward."

Thomas nodded, then asked, "But you said that Prioress Emelyne will ease the tensions between the monks and nuns?"

"She has reason to be more generous. She and Brother Damian, the brother knight who leads the men, came from the same mother's womb. You'll meet him soon enough."

"And she was elected prioress after the murder happened? How odd that greater peace may be born of a crime."

"You heard of the scandal?"

"The old woman who was waiting with us in the hall while…"

The steward laughed. "Ah, but she does love to tell her tales. I was probably asleep when she told you that one. But it was a strange event."

Thomas encouraged him to say more.

"You see, Mistress Hursel, the dead one, was once a high-ranking servant in the household of Prioress Amicia when she was still in the world. First, Mistress Hursel's husband died, then the Lady Amicia's. Soon after, they had some quarrel, and the former prioress dismissed the woman from her service. I don't know why Mistress Hursel came here, but she did and remarried a butcher in this town. Later, Lady Amicia joined the Order and was sent as a nun to Mynchen Buckland, quickly becoming prioress. But the two women had no contact until recently when Mistress Hursel came specifically to visit the prioress. Her second husband had just died."

"In an attempt to make peace, perhaps? Death often makes one ponder whether petty quarrels are worth the grief and sin."

"Poverty also makes one brood. Rumor says that the butcher left his widow with only her legal pittance. His sons took his business, which is prosperous enough, but my wife tells me they have little love for their stepmother."

Thomas wondered whether the woman had come to beg charity. But if refused, she would have been more likely to kill Prioress Amicia, not the reverse. "So no one really knows why Mistress Hursel chose this time to break the silence between them, or even whether the former prioress asked her to come?"

The steward stopped and took a moment to dig a finger into his ear. "The last is unlikely. No rumors say that. As to why Mistress Hursel came, not even Janeta has said, and she served as Prioress Amicia's maid before and after her mistress took vows. My wife heard at the market day, just after the trial, that the maid swore she had announced to her mistress that the butcher's widow was waiting in the cloister to see her. Prioress Amicia went alone to greet the woman. Nothing more."

"A surfeit of dead husbands," Thomas said, and then realized he had spoken his observation aloud.

The steward blinked in confusion.

"I meant only that the rift came after the death of two husbands, while a possible attempt at reconciliation came after the death of another."

"That is a pondering far beyond my ken, Brother. But my wife learned that Mistress Hursel's first husband also left her with nothing much to live on when he died. Seems he had a mistress he supported, but could little afford, so the small farm he owned had to be sold for debts. Then she lost her place in service…" He shrugged.

"Your wife is a wonderful source of information!" Thomas grinned.

"She is not usually prone to chatter, but other women do on market days and she tells us all fine tales over supper." His smile betrayed deep affection for his very helpful wife.

"So Mistress Hursel has had two husbands, both now dead, but barely a roof over her head. Any rumors of a third match?"

The steward shook his head. "None. Even I have heard it said that she became a shrew once the marriage vows were uttered."

The monk nodded. "Was anything else told about the day Mistress Hursel was killed? It must have been a shock to both town and priory."

"It seems that Father Pasche arrived at the priory soon after the dead woman. When Janeta told him about the visitor, he asked to be taken to the garth. I have heard he knew the woman when Prioress Amicia's husband still lived, but why this was so, I never learned."

They were now standing outside the entrance to the building owned by the Hospitaller monks. Thomas knew he had little time to hear what more the steward knew, so he bent to check his foot as if something was amiss with his shoe.

"When Janeta led the priest to the garth, they saw Prioress Amicia bending over the victim and that she had blood all over her hands and robe. It was obvious that Mistress Hursel was dead. When Father Pasche asked the prioress what had happened, she shook her head but said nothing. When he asked her specifically if she had committed the crime, she simply looked at him, then down at the corpse, and refused to defend herself or confess. Father Pasche arranged for her confinement. She was convicted in Chapter, never once contesting the accusation or the evidence. Now she waits for the Prior of England to decree her fate."

"On what evidence was she convicted?" Thomas asked as he stood.

"My wife has heard nothing more, and Janeta never speaks of it to anyone. I assume the priest examined the site. Sister Richolda, the infirmarian, must have seen the corpse. That's what the sheriff and crowner always do. But this was on Church land..." He shook his head. "King's justice or Church authority are equally confusing. Legal matters mean as much as Latin to me, Brother. I know about sheep, not the law."

Thomas was intrigued by the knowledge that the former prioress, victim, and priory priest were acquainted long before the murder took place. He was also troubled that the decision to convict Amicia seemed so swift, yet was so feebly based.

Perhaps Father Pasche knew more about the old quarrel than this steward had learned and had added significant testimony at the trial? If this had cast a strong light on why the prioress might have committed the crime, it did not bode well for proving Amicia innocent.

The steward knocked at the entry door.

It swung open, and a tall monk, the eight-pointed cross displayed like a pure white radiance against the left shoulder of his black robe, stood in the doorway.

"Welcome, Brother Thomas. I am Brother Damian, leader of our small band here. We offer you a warm bed, a hot meal, and any other small comfort you might require in this place dedicated to God's work." He stepped aside and, with graceful invitation, swept his hand toward the interior.

Thomas thanked him and entered, noting as he passed, that Brother Damian was missing his right arm below the elbow.

Chapter Nine

Prioress Eleanor and Sister Anne stood at the window in the chamber they shared.

Eleanor carefully remained to one side, lest someone below see her and conclude that she was able to stand on her injured ankle.

Sister Anne observed the activity in the courtyard. "It is certainly a busy place," she said. "Is it possible that so many local villagers have wares to sell this priory?"

"Can you see if any are invited into the garth?"

Briefly, Anne bent forward, trying hard not to appear overly curious to anyone who might look up at the window and watch her movements. "That is completely hidden from my view." She stepped back.

"Then we can learn nothing from here of value to our purpose."

Anne agreed, then once more looked down at the courtyard. "I wonder if some of those below have come to bring gifts in gratitude for the healing they received at the Order's hospital in Acre."

"Might you also be curious to learn if this priory has any manuscripts brought back from Outremer that remain rare in England?" Eleanor knew her friend collected such treasures and studied them well. Even Queen Eleanor had sent the priory one from Castile for the benefit of Tyndal's hospital.

"Such treasures are more likely found in Clerkenwell's library with the brothers. The infirmarian here is a woman, not a physician, but the nun might have been told some stories about treatments." Anne failed to keep her eagerness hidden. "As I have heard, they used Muslim doctors on occasion in Acre, men who are especially skilled in curing diseases of the eyes."

Eleanor turned away and walked back to the small table where Janeta had recently refilled the ewer of wine and left a small loaf of crusty bread. She put her hand on it and noted that it was still warm from the oven. "This is the first time I have heard a hint of your usual enthusiasm since we left Tyndal."

"I confess my curiosity."

Eleanor poured a little red wine and brought a mazer to her friend. "I have observed how frail you are, as well. Remember the words 'physician, heal thyself'? That admonition suggests to me that healers do not always care well enough for themselves."

"I do not suffer any illness."

Eleanor continued to look at the nun while she sipped her wine in silence.

"I told you I wished to help, and most certainly can do far more to help you solve this murder than peer from a window." Anne had read her friend's quiet but firm gaze well.

"Are you truly strong enough?"

"Any affliction I have experienced lies in melancholia, a disturbance in my humors that I have suffered since my wretched failure to find the causes behind the abbots' deaths at Tyndal last winter."

"It was you who discovered the significant medical facts."

"Not before three men had died."

"One of whom would have died anyway, and the other had sickened before he arrived."

"You are ever charitable, but I expected more of my skills. Pride in them blinded me to the answers."

As Eleanor realized, there was no argument that would soothe her friend, and she chose not to try. Instead, she said, "Your pallor, your thinness, your retreat into prayer and silence…"

"Are the result of melancholia, except for prayer and meditation. Those were an antidote to my wicked pride." The subinfirmarian looked hopefully at her prioress. "It is possible that God has now granted me a way to expiate my sins. If I help you solve this crime, I may redeem myself in His eyes. Consider my assistance as my penance and let me perform it for the good of my soul."

"Your help would be invaluable," Eleanor said with honesty as well as fondness.

"Am I not a simple nun who does not even head the hospital at Tyndal Priory? Of what danger am I, especially if I look as ill as you feared I was?"

Then Eleanor put a cautionary finger to her lips and tiptoed to the door where she bent her head to listen. She shook her head and returned to her friend's side.

Opting nonetheless for prudence, the two women refilled their cups, tore off a portion of the bread, and huddled together as far from the door as possible so their voices would not carry to any unfriendly listener.

"Give me a plan to help you," Anne whispered.

"The body is buried, but the infirmarian is still here. Sister Richolda must have examined it before the Chapter met and offered her opinions as evidence to consider. Perhaps what she noted supported the conclusion that Amicia was the killer. Or perhaps she had unvoiced doubts that she might discuss with you. An innocent consultation between healers would surely not be untoward?"

"I can, with honesty, visit her because I wish to learn from her."

"I must ask Prioress Emelyne for permission, but I think she will grant it. There is nothing suspicious in your desire to learn from the unique experience the Order gained in Outremer. After all, you are a healer, and the healing arts were the reason for the very foundation of the Hospitallers."

"Shall I also explore the site where the murder occurred?"

Eleanor almost said that there would be no value in it but changed her mind. "Yes. Although the cloister garth has been used by many since, and presumably searched for evidence at the time the body was found, I do not know how careful that examination was. If the assumption at the time was that Sister Amicia was the killer, and she refused to claim innocence, any search might well have been perfunctory. Sister Amicia did not say anything about that, if she even knew what had been done. Nor did she tell me who the culprit might have been. That was another question I had no time to ask."

Anne nodded.

"It seems the trial only lasted for the length of one Chapter meeting, so I must conclude that very little testimony was given and nothing of benefit to her."

"I still wonder that no one thought it odd when she would not clearly say that she was guilty."

"Having seen her, I also question why no one doubted her ability to commit the crime. Although I could not determine her age, she is not a young woman. She is clearly frail, but her current state may be the result of her confinement and sorrow." Eleanor sighed. "We have so many questions to answer."

"Then I shall first stroll through the garth at a time when few others might wish to do so," Anne said. "If I am as pale and thin as you say, I can always argue that I am doing so for my health, should anyone ask why I am there."

"Sit often so you can look carefully at the surrounding areas. Few are as good as you are at observing what might be out of place."

Anne was pleased, noting that her friend had finally decided that she might help in this matter. She had won her chance to redeem herself from her earlier failure.

"The bench where Mistress Hursel was killed should still bear traces of her blood," Eleanor said. "You could sit there without anyone thinking it odd. No one would know that you are aware of any details in this tragedy."

"I shall enjoy the opportunity to rid my humors of their dark hue." Anne laughed and then whispered, "I promise discretion. No one will guess what I am really doing."

Eleanor learned back a bit so she could gaze at the sub-infirmarian with mock gravity. "Am I wrong in concluding that you may enjoy our little subterfuge?"

"I think we shall make a good couple in solving this sad crime."

"Haven't we always," Eleanor whispered back.

Chapter Ten

Brother Thomas was given a tiny room close to the chapel. Amused, he stretched out his arms and could almost rest his fingers against the walls. Perhaps if I got up on the bed, I could kneel to pray, he thought, but quickly chastised himself for his lack of gratitude. He doubted anyone but Brother Damian had a larger space.

He was curious about the men who lived in this commandery. Although the Hospitallers were a military Order, and women comprised a small number overall, the nuns here significantly outnumbered the men. Since it was the only female priory of the Order allowed in England, the disparity in numbers was understandable, but it also explained why conflict was inevitable. Unlike the men in the Order of Fontevraud, these monks were not accustomed to taking a mostly subordinate position to women.

Perhaps the tension would ease now that a blood sister and brother ruled the two sides. A brother's wishes invariably ruled over those of any sister, Thomas thought, and then chuckled. Or at least they almost always did. He recalled how his prioress sometimes led her eldest brother to another course of action with subtle suggestions and even jests. Prioress Emelyne might use the same methods with Brother Damian.

Suddenly, his thoughts were cut short by the sound of two men talking just outside his door. His interest sparked, Thomas slipped closer and pressed his ear to the slight gap between door and jamb.

The deeper voice probably belonged to Brother Damian, he decided, the man who had greeted him on arrival.

Despite the brother knight's courteous welcome, Thomas found him disquieting, although he could not precisely define why. The man's missing arm suggested he had been wounded in battle. Such men were often sent home and assigned to lead a commandery where they could further serve the Order by a profitable management of gifted estates. But what was the reason Brother Damian had been given such an inconsequential house to rule? His sister had not been prioress then, so her rank would not have been a factor. Had there been no other commandery available? Had he simply wished to be close to his sister? Was there another cause, and what might it be?

"Our guest will surely be praying now, Brother Martin, but I want you to stay close by him at all times." Brother Damian had chosen to raise his voice.

Thomas knew this was no accident, and he was meant to hear the words. Why, he asked himself, was that necessary?

"Should he wish to visit the women's priory or even send a message to his prioress, come to me at once for direction." Damian cleared his throat. "It is not safe in these marshlands for a stranger to walk without someone to guide him, nor does he know the rules of our Order. We do not wish him to suffer ill fortune, and it is only kindness to prevent him from violating any of our particular rules."

Brother Martin, whose voice was of a higher pitch, swore with impressive eagerness to do as his leader wished.

Thomas wondered why anyone would care if he wanted to visit Prioress Eleanor, something that any other monk or prior would assume was his duty. As for danger, the path to the preceptory might be slick and muddy, but the distance was short. Even a stranger such as he would be unlikely to drown in a mud puddle. If Brother Damian made me vaguely uneasy before, the monk thought, I now have reason to firmly distrust him.

He heard someone walk away. The step was that of a heavier man, and he suspected it must have been Brother Damian who was tall and muscular. But that meant the heretofore unrevealed Brother Martin remained hovering outside his door.

Very well, I shall give him something to do, Thomas decided, and use the opportunity to learn about my newly assigned, and probably very devoted, shadow. Besides, he thought with his hand on the rope latch, I would never want a man to remain idle for no good purpose when he might otherwise find some innocent entertainment or be in the chapel, kneeling in ardent prayer.

He opened the door and stepped outside.

"I am Brother Martin!"

The youth looked too young to shave. His apple-pink cheeks, covered with less down than those of a girl, were round and soft. Otherwise, he was thin, short, and stood before Thomas, panting like a young dog who hopes for a good run with his pack.

I have been assigned a child to spy on me, Thomas decided, then quickly introduced himself to hide his shock. "I am Brother Thomas of the Order of Fontevraud who has accompanied Prioress Eleanor. Your prior has given me this room until she is well enough to return to Tyndal Priory."

The young brother crossed himself with an expression of genuine concern. "Is she ill? I shall pray for her!"

"God is kind. She suffers but was afflicted with a far less severe injury than feared. We were obliged to beg the kindness of your Order's hospitality for a few days until her foot is healed."

"We are honored by your visit," the youth gushed. "We have heard of your exploits on God's behalf."

"Your praise is humbling, but all credit goes to Him. Our duty is to serve His pleasure."

The youth turned scarlet and seemed at a loss for words.

Thomas took pity on him. Brother Martin must have been assigned to watch over him, but this apparent innocent seemed to lack any tiny measure of artifice that even good men owned. And from what the monk had overheard of Brother Damian's orders, the youth might not even realize how nefarious his real task was.

"I wish to stretch my legs after the long ride today." Thomas gestured in the direction of where he believed the fishponds were.

"Do let me accompany you!" The lad stumbled a few steps forward but suddenly halted. He frowned, as if perplexed by a weighty question. Then his eyes shone as he remembered his other directive. "Are you familiar with our Order?"

"Only by reputation, Brother Martin, but I have heard many tales of Hospitaller courage and compassion in Outremer. If your duties allow it, I would enjoy your company and perhaps you can enlighten me on your praiseworthy Order as we walk."

Like a student eager to please his master, Brother Martin once again leapt forth and began a recitation of tales he had heard from Outremer.

Trying not to smile, Brother Thomas decided the youth not only resembled a puppy but owned as much guile as one. He would give the lad something innocuous to report to Brother Damian and thus help him gain a little favor.

As Brother Martin talked, the two men headed to the fishponds which the monk stated he was eager to see. Giving a clear directive seemed to be the best way to deal with his new shadow.

When the youth finished yet another story, he took a deep breath.

Thomas quickly inserted a question. "There seem so few monks in residence," he said. "Some might say the number is not enough to warrant a prior. I mean no criticism. I am simply curious."

Brother Martin blushed, something he seemed inclined to do. "We also feed the steward, whose duties we share with the nuns, and house one priest as well as two lay brothers besides me. Brother Damian is our leader but chooses not to bear the usual title of commander. Because he served as a brother knight in Outremer, however, we all refer to him as our commander to show courtesy."

Not exactly the answer to his question, but Thomas had learned a more interesting detail instead about who lived in the house. "Is that where he lost his lower arm?"

"So I assume, but he never speaks of it."

Thomas nodded, his expression suggesting deep respect. "And have you gone yourself to regain Jerusalem?" This he doubted, but he did not want to insult the boy by making it clear he did not think him capable of a warrior's task.

The young lay brother bowed his head. "I have neither the skills nor stature to do so. I entered the Order because my uncle died in battle there. My family wished it, and I was pleased to so honor him. They appealed to William De Henley, now Prior of England, and offered my insignificant service as a lay brother in his memory. The Prior was kind and granted the plea."

"I have no doubt you will serve God and the Order well, Brother. In spite of our short acquaintance, I have been struck by your dedication." Yet Thomas wondered if the lad had found any vocation either before or after he was given to the Order. Was he even old enough to have suffered a youth's first lust?

Another blush washed the boy's face, and he quickly glanced down.

Brother Martin may be admirably dutiful, Thomas thought, but his reaction to my compliment suggests he has discovered that some vows are not easily kept. He hoped the priest had been kind when the lad explained how his body betrayed him and dreams tempted him beyond endurance.

Still unable to look the monk in the eye, Brother Martin stared ahead and gestured at the view in front of him. "Here are our fishponds," he stammered. "I think you will find them superior to most. If pride were not wicked, we might boast of them."

As Thomas had noted on arrival, the ponds were large, but now he could see how badly they needed tending. Noxious pond weeds fouled them, thick bands of tangled vegetation stretching into the water like gnarled fingers. The path along the perimeter was slippery with mud. In several places, the earth had crumbled, and sediment dyed the water with a gloomy hue.

"Surely Brother Damian has plans to improve them further?" the monk asked, looking back at the youth. Was he mistaken or had the shadow of a troubling emotion bleached the color from Brother Martin's face? Was the pallor caused by a passing sadness? Might it even be a stronger one—like fear?

The young man bit his lip, and the moment fled as quickly as it had arrived. "I am sure that Prioress Emelyne, now that she rules the nuns, will share much more bounty from their rents with us. Brother Damian is her elder brother."

"I did not know their relationship!" A small enough lie, Thomas thought, and perhaps not even worthy of confession, considering the purpose for which it was uttered. "Then the conviction of Prioress Amicia for the murder of ..." He shook his head. "I fear I heard only a little about her guilt in this tragedy while we waited to be greeted by Prioress Emelyne."

"Mistress Hursel was the corpse." Brother Martin nervously checked the immediate area as if worried a ghost might be lurking.

"Ah, yes. That must have shocked you all." Once again, Thomas saw the lad turn pale and he wondered if this had been caused solely by the lad's horror over murder done on sacred ground. Silently, he chided himself for being so eager to discover information that his imagination was beginning to dominate his reason.

A gull passing overhead uttered a strident cry.

Brother Martin looked away but did not reply to the monk's comment.

The young man must have been startled by the bird, Thomas forced himself to conclude. Nothing more. He continued, "Yet despite that misfortune, some good has emerged. It seems the elevation of your commander's sister to lead Mynchen Buckland will be a blessing to the monks."

"The fishponds are used by both nuns and brothers, but, as I have heard, Prioress Amicia often sent more money than was her responsibility to the Prior of England for the benefit of Outremer and ignored some needs for improvements in our buildings, especially if they remained serviceable." He looked at the ponds and sighed. "One of the other lay brothers and I had to shore up parts of the rim with rocks over there where the earth had slid into the water." He gestured in the direction of the road that led into the priory. "We did so after a villager was badly injured when the path collapsed under his feet."

"Prioress Amicia's desire to send more to Clerkenwell must have been hard to accept when Brother Damian saw work here that needed attention."

"Prioress Amicia was a virtuous woman, most devoted to the causes God favored." This time the explanation for his grey hue was clear. "Or so we thought until she was convicted of this murder."

"I meant no reproach, for I am not acquainted with her nor did I know her reputation. I only meant that it may be best for all if Prioress Emelyne is more willing to accept the direction her brother offers."

"Yes," Brother Martin said and sighed with evident relief.

"Yet surely the murder has troubled you all, as it would in our priory at Tyndal."

Brother Martin stiffened like a student about to recite a lesson that had required a long and difficult memorization. "Brother Damian may have been pleased at the elevation of his sister to head the nuns' preceptory, but it grieved him that the former prioress was convicted. Her husband had been his close friend and, as rumor has it, once saved his life. They fought together in Outremer. When he died, Brother Damian spent hours in the chapel praying."

Thomas could barely control his curiosity. "A friend of the husband?"

Brother Martin nodded. "It was also her lord husband who urged the Prior of England to appoint Brother Damian commander here so he would have the comfort of his sister, who was then a nun in the nearby preceptory."

From this dutiful recitation, Brother Thomas wondered how much of the speech had been meant for his specific ears. Even though he was eager to learn more, he knew he must be guarded with his questions. If he were wise, he would ask nothing else. Brother Martin could tell the commander that he had inquired about the crime but was satisfied with the permitted information. Let the child spy receive praise and Damian be content.

There was another reason Thomas chose to be prudent. This youth might seem guileless, but innocence could be cleverly feigned.

In appearance, the lad was almost feminine. In speech and demeanor, he seemed to lack a sharp wit. But clever spies often presented themselves as less dangerous than they were. Brother Damian knew his chosen spy well. Thomas did not.

The monk smiled and turned his questions back to the plans to improve the fishponds. His instinct might continue to insist that it would not take much to outwit this man-child, but he opted to obey the more circumspect voice of his experience.

Chapter Eleven

One look around the cloister garth and Sister Anne lost hope of searching unnoticed.

The garden was being well-tended that morning by nuns and lay sisters alike. Even on this damp spring day, several were on their knees, pulling weeds and otherwise joyfully engaged in convincing life to return to the earth. Some worked in the dirt because the results reminded them of the Resurrection. Others seemed to find tranquility in the prayerful act of tending God's creation.

But all this activity and the normal use of the cloister as a place to exercise, talk companionably, or even meet with visitors were not conducive to finding crucial evidence in a murder investigation.

Nonetheless, Sister Anne diligently sauntered along the paths with head solemnly bowed to discourage any who might be eager to engage a stranger from another religious Order in conversation. With eyes fixed on the ground, she concentrated on seeking any detail, no matter how small, that might have been missed. Success was an unlikely hope, but she was determined.

May God forgive me for this dishonest attitude of prayer, she thought. Surely He knows no ill is meant, only a desire for justice. In that achievement, my longing for His blessing is sincere.

Her deception succeeded.

Two nuns passed her by but said nothing until they thought they were far enough away. Anne's sharp hearing picked up the murmured observation: "She came with Prioress Eleanor of Tyndal, you know. Did you see how gaunt and pale she is? We may be wise to avoid her company lest she carry a contagion."

Perhaps my melancholia has finally served me well, the sub-infirmarian thought, and fought off a telltale smile.

Walking slowly with no seeming direction to forestall any suspicion that she had a destination in mind, Sister Anne spied the discolored bench to her right where Mistress Hursel's body had been found. To add further support to the conclusion that she was ill, she braced herself against the stone bench and eased herself down to sit, then looked heavenward and sighed with evident relief.

The bench might still be stained with faded blood, but she was certain the weapon had vanished long ago if it had not been recovered at the time the corpse was found. From the churned up earth around her feet, Anne knew that many others had since passed by here, after the shock of the murder had vanished, and probably sat on the bench, despite the reddish mark. If a clue had been left, it was buried in the mud, destroyed by many feet, tossed aside as trash, or even innocently picked up as a curiosity.

She turned her thoughts to how the murderer might have killed the victim.

From what the former prioress had told Eleanor, the body remained seated on the bench. It was not until it was touched that Amicia had realized Mistress Hursel was dead. The body began to fall forward, as Anne recalled the tale, and the former prioress grabbed it, thus getting blood on her hands and robe.

A nun passed by with a handful of garden implements. She hesitated, glanced at Sister Anne, and her concerned eyes asked a silent question.

The sub-infirmarian responded with a thin smile and lowered her head contemplatively as if musing in prayer.

The woman walked on.

Anne carefully inched toward the stain and looked around under half-closed eyelids.

If the victim was sitting when attacked, she thought, the killer must have come from behind her. But Anne saw little space behind the bench, where a naked shrub with thorny branches grew, and certainly not enough to allow someone to sneak up without being noticed.

Another conclusion might be that Mistress Hursel was seated, and the killer had approached her from the front. But if that were so, wouldn't the victim have risen when greeted by the prioress, a woman whose husband had been of high enough rank to include a baron amongst his friends? Did that suggest the killer was known by the butcher's widow to be her social equal or even of lower status? The victim would not have stood for a lay brother or sister, for instance, but surely she would also have risen for the priest.

If the killer had struck down Mistress Hursel while she stood, she would have fallen to the ground or backwards against the bench, not into a sitting position on it. The condemned prioress maintained the corpse was seated on the bench and seemed to be musing with her head lowered or else she was asleep. In an area where people often walked, it was unlikely the killer would have taken the time to lift and pose the corpse. If the body had fallen to the ground, it would have been left there.

Had Amicia's story to Prioress Eleanor about the position of the corpse been told to the nuns at the trial? If so, the priest had not contradicted her. Had the infirmarian testified? Anne knew all that should be resolved. What questions were asked and what were the responses? It would also be important to know what was not asked and why.

Leaning back to study the area just behind the bench more closely, Anne saw no signs of footprints. The ground close to the shrub had been cleaned of weeds and dead leaves, however, and she did not know when that had been done. Considering the busy crew of monastic gardeners today, was it likely they had just weeded this patch? Or had the rains prevented performing all the usual tasks? Unless she asked, which she dared not if she wished to be circumspect, she would not know.

The sub-infirmarian sighed, concluding that her prioress had been right and there was nothing to find here.

Just as she decided to leave, a brief ray of light burst through the clouds. Out of the corner of her eye, Anne thought she saw a flash of color behind the bench in a tangle of small stems extending from the lower part of the shrub.

She carefully looked around, saw no one close enough by to see her, and plunged her hand into the mulch of decayed leaves and other vegetation around the trunk itself that had either been missed or deliberately left by the gardeners.

Biting her lip to keep from crying out, she realized there was good reason why no one had cleaned that small area. Sharp thorns pricked her hand, but she ignored them and clutched a handful of earth where she thought the item lay hidden.

The object was small but hard. Opening her hand, the soil fell away to reveal a small gold ring. The band was a popular stirrup shape, and it was topped with a deep red almandine garnet. As she again closed her hand over it, she wondered if it was a clue or if it had been lost by a nun or some visitor. Hospitaller nuns were allowed some minor possessions, and such a ring, albeit one made of gold, would be permitted.

Her thoughts went back to how Mistress Hursel might have been struck. It must have been from behind while she was seated, she thought, otherwise how could the corpse have remained in that position? But to do so the killer must have been standing behind the victim near the shrub. Why would the murderer have been so close to the victim? Could the ring have been lost then?

She twisted around to look, trying to calculate where the killer must have stood and if the ring could have fallen where she had found it.

"Sister Anne!"

The sub-infirmarian started and almost dropped the ring but managed to keep her hand firmly closed over it.

Standing in front of her, an agitated Janeta stared at her with wide eyes.

Sister Anne stood, trying to brush her hand against her robe to clean off some of the obvious dirt. "Is Prioress Eleanor taken ill?"

"No, but I have been searching everywhere for you," the maid replied. "I wondered if you would like a tour of this priory. As someone who belongs to another Order, Prioress Emelyne thought you might find some aspects of the preceptory interesting."

The sub-infirmarian accepted the offer with warm enthusiasm, and, when Janeta turned her back, she slipped the ring into the pouch at her waist.

Of course, the tour might prove useful in suggesting clues or ideas for further investigation, Anne thought, but a little voice nibbled at her. Was the invitation a simple matter of hospitality or was Prioress Emelyne hoping to keep her too busy to wander unsupervised?

Chapter Twelve

Prioress Emelyne stood by the Prioress of Tyndal's bed, her face carefully arranged into an expression of suitable compassion.

A silent nun remained by the door.

Hands folded modestly over her furred cover, Eleanor smiled sweetly but was not deceived by the almost flawless portrayal of concern presented by the Hospitaller leader.

Cautiously studying the woman, she noted that Emelyne's eyes swept the room, resting briefly here and there if something seemed amiss. She understood why the nuns might choose her as their leader. Prioress Emelyne seemed competent, observant, and bore herself with confidence. As a religious leader should do, she probably inspired just a little awe. Indeed, Eleanor might be tempted to choose her as her own sub-prioress, were she one of Tyndal's nuns.

Yet she did not trust her.

She had seen hints of rage and wondered if there was a bit of cruelty in her soul. Although Emelyne was probably close to Eleanor in age, she already had deep furrows between her brows, and in her forehead, but none around her mouth. This was not a woman much prone to laughter.

Were I in her charge and guilty of even the smallest transgression, Eleanor thought, I would tremble with fear. Yet here I lie, engaged in a deception, and feel neither shame nor trepidation.

With a hint of amusement, she admitted to God that the cause was probably her wicked pride. Whatever earthly flaws this troubling prioress owned, she was unmistakably clever, and Eleanor found herself eager to match wits with her in whatever chess game Prioress Emelyne was playing. But she also knew this was no lighthearted sport. If Amicia was innocent, a murderer was loose. Might this prioress own any guilt in the matter?

"I am grateful for your kind hospitality and assigning Janeta to help Sister Anne with my care. That was most charitable," Eleanor said. And she offered these appreciative words with an honest smile. After the initial delay in greeting them, the prioress had provided well for their needs.

Prioress Emelyne bowed her head. "As God directs us to do good works, it is He who deserves all thanks." The woman's smile might own little warmth, but her words were softly spoken. "I see that your sub-infirmarian is not here. Do you have need for anything until she returns?"

"Sister Anne's health suffered during our journey to visit my brother and then our travel here. Since I have heard that your cloister gardens soothe the eye and spirit even in the dark seasons, I granted her permission to take some exercise there." To lend credibility, Eleanor had learned long ago, it was always wise to be as truthful as possible in the midst of deceit.

With relief, the prioress saw no unease in Emelyne's expression. Not that there was any reason why Sister Anne should not walk in the cloister, as many others must have since the murder, but she would have been interested if this prioress had revealed concern.

Instead, Emelyne walked over to the window, briefly gazed down at the view of the busy courtyard, and then turned back to her guest. "Did you learn from our former prioress why your most generous brother insisted you give the charter only to her? I confess curiosity. Elder brothers are, as you noted, disinclined to explanations." She laughed.

Her laughter is believable, but her smile was patently not, Eleanor thought as she nodded in sympathetic response. "It is so often hard not to question the brother who heads the family, being the curious creatures we are." Not that she hadn't quarreled with Hugh, and even found ways to circumvent her father's edicts when he was alive, but a wise woman did not confide such things in casual conversation.

"Do you not find this room has a chill?" Emelyne gestured to the nun, and the woman went immediately to the ewer of wine.

An interesting and very swift change of subject, Eleanor thought. "This warm coverlet you had placed on my bed chases away all coldness," Eleanor replied and refused the offer of wine.

Emelyne sipped her mazer, her eyes watching her guest over the rim of the cup.

A heavy silence fell in the chamber.

A good stratagem to make me say more about my conversation with the former prioress while appearing to be interested only in my brother's bequest, Eleanor concluded. In silence, she acknowledged with appreciation the skill of her fellow prioress. In this instance, she would yield, taking to heart the maxim about minor concessions and losses lulling an adversary into complaisance. It was her brother's maxim about war, but Eleanor found it was equally true in the battles of wits.

"My brother knew your former prioress in the days before she took vows," she said to Emelyne. "Or at least he knew her husband. The two men went to Outremer to fight for Jerusalem, although they did not do so together. That is a kinship that breeds strong loyalties. Perhaps it is the reason he wished the widow to receive the gift."

Emelyne betrayed relief. "Then the baron might also have known of our hospital work."

"I discovered after his return that he had been wounded. He may well have benefited from your Order's healing talents in Acre."

Once again, the Prioress of Mynchen Buckland turned her attention to the window and stared silently down at the courtyard.

"Sister Amicia was well pleased when I told her of the gift," Eleanor said and now wondered if the woman was staring out the window to make sure exactly what could and could not be seen from it.

"How did she seem to you?" Emelyne kept her back turned so her expression remained hidden.

But Eleanor noticed a slight tremor in her voice. She chose to reply truthfully. "She is gaunt, spends her hours in prayer, and appears to suffer profound sorrow."

When Emelyne did face her guest, Eleanor was surprised to see a slight glistening on her cheeks.

"Did she tell you that she is dying?"

Eleanor gasped. This was not what she had expected to hear. "She said nothing of that. From what does she suffer?"

"Long before this tragic murder, I had observed that she was in increasing ill health. Yet, despite the signs, she had not sought treatment. One day, she collapsed, weeping in terrible pain. It must have become unbearable or she would not have betrayed such weakness. Sister Richolda, our infirmarian, was allowed to examine her and found a large tumor in her breast. In her experience, such a growth has no cure. Now she visits our former prioress weekly and supplies a drink infused with the poppies of Lethe to ease our prisoner's mortal suffering until death takes her soul."

"And so, mortally ill, she may soon be cast forth naked into the world for her crime?" Eleanor kept her tone blandly factual.

"After we had judged her guilty of the murder, and I was elected prioress, I sent the trial report to the Prior of England and included the news of her imminent death. I begged him to allow her to remain here, in her current cell, where she may be treated with compassion and die in peace. Before she committed this crime, she had served our Order well and was known for piety. I believe the Prior will find that mercy is warranted. It has long been our practice to treat the mortal ills of all with compassion. God demands it."

For the first time, Eleanor felt a twinge of guilt. Prioress Emelyne was showing admirable mercy. The Hospitallers had long been known for treating everyone equally who sought their healing, not caring about the faith of the sufferer or their status in the world. But to do so for a convicted murderer?

Once again, she wondered if Amicia had tricked her with a clever story because of her dead husband's friendship with Hugh. Yet Eleanor remained convinced by her tale. Statements were made at the trial but never properly challenged. Many questions should have been pursued but were not. After many years reading the souls of men and women alike, she was not prone to falling for deceptions.

No, she thought, I remain determined to do what I am able to discover the truth. Then she asked, "Does your former prioress know that you have begged this mercy on her behalf?"

"I told her. She knows the high regard with which we all previously held her. She thanked me for the clemency, then begged me to let her stay in solitude with God, as penance for her many sins. I told her I would honor that and visit only when she requested it. She sees Father Pasche, but I fear I will see her again only on her deathbed."

"I wonder that a woman so ill would have the strength to kill another?"

Emelyne stiffened, her eyes glittering with an odd light.

Eleanor knew she had erred and quickly added, "But she has confessed, and no one who is innocent would ever go to God's judgment with a lie on her lips."

It took a moment, but Emelyne visibly calmed. She sipped the wine again and looked away.

Yet Eleanor noted she did not say that Amicia had never actually confessed to the crime.

And this detail was important. It was one reason Eleanor believed that Amicia was speaking the truth about her innocence. Another reason was that she would tell the priest whether or not she bore any guilt in her final confession. The fate of her soul demanded it. So if she was as close to death as Prioress Emelyne believed, why beg someone to prove her innocent if she were not? Amicia knew that she could remain here under a gentle confinement and die in relative comfort. There was no logical reason to pursue a different verdict unless the woman was not guilty of this crime.

As she watched Emelyne hand her empty mazer to the silent nun, she wondered if Hugh had known of Amicia's fatal illness and that was why he had written that personal letter to her.

"Should you wish for anything," Prioress Emelyne said, now clearly eager to return to her duties, "please send Janeta, and I will comply."

"Then I would beg one small favor now," Eleanor said. "Your Order has gained much knowledge about healing in Outremer. Sister Anne, as my sub-infirmarian, would benefit from this. Might she spend some time with Sister Richolda and follow her on her rounds with patients? Our priory would be deeply grateful for anything she might learn."

"A wish I am delighted to grant," Emelyne replied. "Sister Richolda once served in Outremer, before she took vows, being one of the last women to work in the hospital. Her work was primarily with women giving birth but she has also, to our benefit, learned other skills that make her a great comfort to the sick here."

Eleanor bowed her head as she expressed her gratitude.

But as Prioress Emelyne started to leave, she stopped and turned back. "Your sub-infirmarian may also go with Sister Richolda when she visits our former prioress. But you should know that Janeta always accompanies her to tend to whatever small needs her former mistress requires. With your nun and the maid gone, you should not be alone. Send Janeta with word, and I shall send a lay sister to sit by your bedside."

With that, she and the nun swept out the door.

Eleanor felt certain she had just been checkmated in this game the two women were playing, yet she was unable to define exactly how.

"I admire Prioress Emelyne's skill," she murmured to the empty room, and then her grey eyes grew dark with determination. "The Hospitaller prioress may have won this match, but she will not win the next."

Chapter Thirteen

Sister Richolda studied her visitor with a critical eye.

Sister Anne returned the wordless greeting in like fashion, noting that the infirmarian may have been elderly but her eyes were clear. The thin face was deeply lined and her back slightly bent. What caught Anne's attention next were her knotted fingers.

"Which I can use easily enough," the infirmarian announced, noting the focus of the sub-infirmarian's gaze and raising one hand. Her eyes twinkled with humor and approval.

"There is little you fail to observe," Anne replied with a smile.

"It would be wicked pride if I concurred, Sister, but you are free to hold any opinion you wish." She first glanced at Janeta, who stood by the entry to the apothecary, then turned back to her shelves of potions and jars. With a light touch, she ran her fingers over the containers, selected a couple, and set them down on a nearby table.

"During our short stay here, I would be grateful if I might learn a little from your experience," Anne said. "I have been told that you gained much medical wisdom in Acre."

Sister Richolda continued to concentrate on her medicines. "You may be disappointed, Sister. I am only the widow of a poor English crusader who died of a rotting wound in Outremer. With no funds or family, I was forced to beg the Hospitallers for charity, and they chose to let me serve mothers who had just given birth in their hospital."

"Yet you learned all this." Anne gestured around the small room.

"God's ways are mysterious, indeed! Soon after I arrived, a midwife, who was also skilled in herbs, came to treat one of the young mothers who suffered a fever. She watched as I spoke with the nursing women and carried their babes to them from the wee cots near their beds. That day, she asked that I be allowed to assist her in small matters when she came. Out of merciful kindness, she taught me much about the care of women."

Sister Anne was intrigued but remained silent, hoping Richolda would tell more of the story.

The infirmarian looked over her shoulder. "Women cared for the men only as cooks or servants. When my service was not needed for the mothers, I made beds, emptied and cleaned chamber pots, or brought blankets, food, and water to the men who lay in the hospital. There was one doctor, a Jew, who was respected by our Christian physicians for his skill with wounds. I do not know why he did this, but, if some small task required attention, he always gestured to me to do it. Often he came with a student and, while he taught the young man, he insisted that I remain nearby to bring him things he needed. By then, I was fascinated by the healing arts, and I memorized every word he uttered."

Remembering how her own father had often required her help when he taught, Sister Anne smiled.

"In time, I chose to take Hospitaller vows as a lay sister, returned to England, and then to this priory. For some years, I helped the infirmarian here and learned more from her. When she died, our prioress found me worthy enough to take her place."

She set another jar down on the table, folded her hands, and tilted her head. "How came you to your skills?"

"My father was a physician and taught me what he knew. Later, I became an apothecary with my husband before he chose to serve God and I followed him into the Order of Fontevraud."

Sister Richolda looked at her with surprise and evident curiosity. "A father who taught his daughter the art of healing?"

"He had no son."

"That doesn't explain his decision, child. He must have loved you dearly."

The use of the word *child* amused Anne, now decades past the age when it would have applied, but she knew the word was meant gently and the nun's age gave her the right. Anne simply bowed her head in silent humility.

"I know your reputation, Sister. He taught you well. Tyndal Priory's hospital is known across the land for healing skill."

"Sister Christina is the infirmarian there. I only assist her."

"Many speak of her saintliness, a woman whose prayers soothe the suffering and often heal, but it is your name that is spoken with awe."

Blushing, Anne replied, "I have much to learn, Sister."

"I doubt my small skills will teach you anything you do not know, but I have a patient you may wish to see while I treat her. She suffers from festering teeth. I have removed them and packed her mouth with linen wads infused with a little milky sap from wild lettuce. While she heals, she has slept a great deal but feels little pain."

Anne's face brightened with interest.

Sister Richolda beckoned her to follow, and the two nuns walked into the small room adjacent to the apothecary where two patients lay in narrow cots.

The forgotten Janeta doggedly followed.

With mild interest, Sister Richolda noted this but quickly turned her attention to the nuns awaiting her care.

The first patient was a younger nun. Sister Richolda introduced her companion, explaining that she was the healer from another Order, and told Sister Anne that this was the nun whose teeth had been extracted.

Her cheeks bulging with linen wads, the patient could only nod at the tall visitor.

Opening the woman's mouth and sitting down to examine it, Richolda looked pleased. "You are almost well," she said, "and may be released to your duties tomorrow." She extracted a few wads.

"God has blessed me with little pain," the woman mumbled. "I must offer Him my gratitude."

Sister Richolda heartily agreed and then rose. As they walked away, she bent close to Anne's ear. "I find that the sick heal faster if not in pain," she whispered. "I overheard that from a Hospitaller doctor in Acre. He told his student that he had learned it from a Muslim physician, but that God had never punished him for following the advice."

Anne whispered back, "Nor has He struck me down for washing my hands after each patient as my father taught me."

Raising an eyebrow, Richolda replied, "Your father either went on pilgrimage to Outremer or he was an unusual physician."

"He was well-read," Anne replied and fell silent.

As they approached a nun of later years, Anne noticed that she lay stiffly on her bed, her eyes narrowed and her lips pinched.

Sister Richolda gently raised the nun into a sitting position, and then checked her back and sides.

Anne thought she saw something bulky under the nun's habit.

"Have you gotten any relief?" The infirmarian raised the woman's face and studied her eyes.

"I came to you screaming in agony, Sister. Now I only ache, but the current pain is one I can endure with the aid of fervent prayer."

"Perhaps an adjustment in the infusion I have ordered..."

"It makes me nauseous. I do not like it. It is a devilish thing, and I refuse more." Carefully twisting from side to side, she winced, then she bent forward and smiled. "As you see, I am able to bow to God and need not see what happens to my left or right as long as I can keep the cross in view."

"Then return to your prayers," Richolda replied, "although I shall send word to Prioress Emelyne that you must be excused from any duty requiring the lifting of heavy weights. Perhaps you could sit and polish some of the items that rest on the altar and have been given to us for the glory of God."

As the woman rose with a little assistance and trod carefully on her way out the door, Sister Anne bent toward the infirmarian's ear. "What was your treatment?"

"A brace for her back. One of the doctors used such a thing in Acre for a man with a spinal injury. Sadly, I was unable to see exactly how it was constructed, but it seemed to bring relief. When this nun came to me, I had no ease for her except poppy juice, which, as you heard, she abhorred. My awkward effort with splints and bands has not healed her, but she is, for the moment, content."

"Theodoric of Bologna," Sister Anne said. "He wrote of using splints and plaster to support necks and spines."

Sister Richolda straightened with excitement. "You have tried this method?"

"Never, nor have I seen it used before. Your patient looks remarkably free of pain. I am eager to learn more about your brace."

"Then we shall talk about the treatment after I see what supplies I might need to replenish." The infirmarian went to the shelf in the infirmary, where she kept already-prepared infusions and pastes, and peered into jars and boxes.

Anne glanced at Janeta and noted the maid's face had turned a sickly green. Concerned, she asked if she were well.

"Forgive me," the maid replied. "I must visit the garderobe!"

"Shall I accompany you?"

Janeta shook her head and fled.

Noting the departing maid, Sister Richolda finished her inventory, took her guest by the arm, and guided her back to the apothecary. "I know you have questions for me," she said, "and not all of them are about Outremer and braces."

Chapter Fourteen

Sister Richolda held up a cautioning hand as she went back to the door and looked down the hall.

Sister Anne used the opportunity to praise her. "Your ability to learn so much with little instruction continues to astonish me."

Richolda turned around and smiled. "Apart from the extended kindness of the midwife in Acre and the infirmarian here, I often listened in silence to the conversations of men because I suffer that woman's vice of curiosity. God also gave me the gift of remembering everything I see and hear. When an emergency occurred in the maternity ward, and no one of acknowledged skill was there, I sometimes treated the suffering one. Yet I never spoke of my effort if the woman lived. It was God's will if she did, and equally His if she did not."

Anne nodded understanding. When she and her husband had their apothecary shop, Anne stayed in his shadow, although it was she who had been trained by a physician. When they both entered Tyndal Priory, however, he had dropped all pretense of expertise while she had offered her gifts to the hospital there.

Sister Richolda closed the door and faced her fellow healer. "Now for those questions on other matters that concern you. Ask, while we may be free to discuss them." Her previously light tone was replaced with solemnity.

Anne wavered for an instant. Could she trust this woman enough to ask about Mistress Hursel? Yet to ignore the infirmarian's offer might banish any hope she had of learning needed information. In an attempt not to betray her fear of blundering, she phrased her interest as something one inquiring woman could ask of another who had just confessed to the vice of inquisitiveness.

"I am curious about the murder that took place here. We were quite shocked that Prioress Amicia had been convicted of the crime. My prioress had expected to meet with her."

Gesturing to the bench near the shelves filled with medicine, Sister Richolda sat and Anne joined her.

Anne noted that the infirmarian faced the entryway.

Sister Richolda massaged her knuckles as if they pained her. "It stunned us, and I was horrified when the body was brought here for my examination."

"Forgive me. I have no purpose for inquiring into these matters, but I also own that woman's frailty of succumbing to the vice of curiosity."

"Then let us both indulge in the wickedness. I suspect it would be deemed a minor sin in this instance."

Anne smiled.

But the infirmarian returned it with a troubled, almost pleading expression. "The poor woman was probably killed by a knife thrust into her chest. The wound was both narrow and shallow, most probably caused by a common dining tool which can be lethal if enough force is used. The blow was well-placed. It entered here." She pointed to her heart. "And, if I am correct and the scratches on her breast were new, the knife was driven up to the hilt which might have left those marks. It would have taken a strong blow, perhaps made with two hands, especially because the angle suggests it was done from behind."

Choosing not to interrupt this rapid flow of words, Anne only raised a puzzled eyebrow.

"Had she been struck from the front, the angle would not have been as sharp unless the assailant was of remarkable height. As you might also ask, I was surprised that Prioress Amicia could have found the strength. She has suffered of late from a marked frailty." Richolda caught her breath as if stopping herself from saying more.

"Yet she was convicted of the murder," Anne said, eager to hear the response.

The infirmarian looked down at her lap.

"Was your testimony required in Chapter?"

Sister Richolda gripped her hands. Her knuckles grew white, and she nodded once.

"Were you asked about her frailty?"

"It was I who mentioned it. In response, Father Pasche reminded us all that the Devil bestows great strength on sinners when he fills them with rage. Then he asked me whether she might have been able to kill if the Evil One had thus taken over her soul. I could not deny the likelihood."

"Am I correct in thinking you were not completely swayed by his argument?" Anne asked the question with a sympathetic tone.

"Prioress Amicia was a good woman, yet many of us were confused by her manner during the trial. If it was not the Evil One who had possessed her and made her commit the crime, why not deny her guilt? If she was guilty, why not confess? I do not understand why she did neither. The guiltless proclaim their innocence. The nuns had little choice but to convict her." A tear crested and fell down her cheek. "I refused to vote."

Those words were barely audible as if she were either ashamed or frightened by her decision to abstain. The infirmarian may not have directly answered her question, but Anne was certain the abstention signified her doubt of the woman's guilt. "It must have grieved everyone that your former prioress had done this vile act."

"Many of us continue to weep for her, although none doubt that Prioress Emelyne will prove a worthy successor."

"You said that she was *probably* killed by a knife. Was the weapon not recovered?"

"It was not in the body at the time the murder was discovered. Neither Father Pasche nor Brother Damian thought it necessary to look for it as Prioress Amicia had accepted guilt. Although the sheriff was summoned and informed of all proceedings, the perpetrator was under Church authority and he had no further need to be involved. But a small knife was found by a nun not long afterward. It lay just under a layer of dead leaves near the bench. No one was certain it was the weapon, nor was the owner ever found. Identification of such a common item is usually impossible."

"Did your former prioress explain why the knife was not left in the body?"

"When asked, she said only that she remembered nothing about it."

Anne heard footsteps behind her.

Sister Richolda smiled sympathetically. "Do you feel better, my child, or do you need a remedy from my supply?"

Anne stood and noted that Janeta's color was no longer green.

"Thank you, Sister. I need nothing. My courses are due, and I often feel ill before they arrive. I am now well."

"Then I am sure you and Sister Anne will have other parts of the priory to visit." Sister Richolda stood and folded her hands.

There was nothing else that Anne wished to see of Mynchen Buckland, and she wondered how she could find a way to spend additional time with this infirmarian. What she had already learned from the woman's tumble of words suggested there was more to find out.

As if Sister Richolda had read her mind, she quickly said, "Perhaps you and I can visit again soon. I long to hear what else you have learned from Theodoric of Bologna about the use of braces for necks and spines, Sister." Her eyes now shone with a pleasant thought. "Come with me on my next visit to our former prioress!" She glanced at the maid. "Janeta and I visit her weekly. Sister Amicia suffers a sad illness, and you might find the treatment of interest. With her maid there, she will surely feel more comfortable, and I would be grateful for your opinion. Would you be willing to consult in this matter?"

With proper humility, Sister Anne readily agreed, and the two nuns decided on the time for the visit.

• ● ● ● •

As she and Janeta walked away, Anne mulled over what the infirmarian had told her.

It was noteworthy that the priest had pointedly directed the nuns to a guilty verdict. He might just as easily have emphasized the unlikelihood that Amicia had done anything more than find the body. When Brother Thomas came to visit, Prioress Eleanor could ask him to find out more about Father Pasche.

Sister Richolda's willingness to tell her about her observations of the corpse was also interesting. Her demeanor suggested that she was deeply troubled by the verdict, her own role in the nuns' decision, or perhaps both. Since she seemed eager to meet again, Anne would find a way to explore this aspect more thoroughly.

But there was one more detail that intrigued her. The infirmarian did not want to discuss any details of her examination in Janeta's hearing. Was it consideration for the loyal maid whose mistress had been condemned for murder? Was there another reason?

Surely Sister Richolda's testimony that Amicia had been too frail to commit the crime would have given comfort to the servant. She would have no need to hide those thoughts from the maid.

Anne shook her head with bewilderment. It was medicine she cared about, not confusing investigations into the motives for murder, but she owed God penance for her sins last winter. At least He had been kind enough to allow her to share knowledge with this skillful infirmarian who had gained wisdom from those at the hospital in Acre. That, by itself, was worth the hard journey here.

Chapter Fifteen

Sister Anne felt the area around Eleanor's ankle.

The prioress dutifully gasped in pain.

"Please report to Prioress Emelyne that the ankle is not as swollen but that Prioress Eleanor remains unable to put weight on her injured foot." With a brief glance at Janeta, the sub-infirmarian began to rewrap the ankle with a fresh herbal poultice which included pounded marshmallow root from Sister Richolda's supply.

The maid left the room and shut the door firmly behind her.

Taking care to walk silently, Anne hurried to the door, listened, then opened it a little so it would not squeak.

The maid's footsteps were fading down the hall.

Cautiously closing the door, Sister Anne turned and chuckled as she saw Prioress Eleanor already out of bed and pacing the room.

"This inaction is intolerable! I pray for the patience to keep me from revealing my stratagem."

"It is the only way we can succeed," Anne replied and then quickly reached out to grasp her friend's arm. "Stay away from the window!"

Eleanor laughed. "You know me well." With a longing glance at the opened shutters, she stepped back.

"I have an item to show you that may dampen your impatience and prove the wisdom of your plan."

Eleanor stopped pacing. "You have found something?"

Sister Anne handed her the delicate ring. "I found this under a shrub behind the bench where Mistress Hursel was found slain. The bush is thorny, and thus the area closest to the roots had not been cleared of dead vegetation."

Eleanor studied it with a frown. "A fine piece of work, yet we cannot know to whom it belonged nor how it came to be in that place." With a gentle touch, she ran her finger over the dark red stone.

"It might be meaningful." Anne sounded disappointed.

"I agree. As I thought more on it, I realized that any search of the area would not have been thorough. All believed they had the killer when Prioress Amicia did not deny she had committed the crime."

"The ring is unbroken."

"Therefore we may conclude it did not break and fall off. Yet the band is thin. Someone either wore the ring often or over many years. If so, it must have been a treasured item." She held it up to the stronger light. "See here. The band is slightly bent. And the size could only fit a small finger. A woman's ring, most likely." Eleanor gave it back to Anne. "Was someone wearing it? If so, why did it fall off? If it was not worn, why did the person carry it with them? And how? In a pouch?" She hesitated for a moment. "And why was it not recovered before you found it?"

"Might it have been pulled off in a struggle between the killer and Mistress Hursel?"

"If there had been time for a struggle," Eleanor replied, "Mistress Hursel would have cried out." She gazed at the ring resting in her friend's palm. "I fear it is more likely to have belonged to someone other than the victim or her killer. A nun might have kept it in a pouch, if, for example, it was a gift from a beloved family member. To wear that precious stone would be unsuitable for one now vowed to God. And the garnet suggests the giver possessed some status and wealth." She smiled briefly. "It interests me that the jewel is red, the color most associated with selfless love, the blood of martyrs, and also redemption."

"Then it may have belonged to Prioress Amicia."

Eleanor nodded. "As for Mistress Hursel, I doubt it was hers. The ring is too fine to belong to a woman who had been a servant unless she held a special place in the family's heart. That is unlikely in this instance. The woman had been dismissed after a quarrel with her mistress."

"So it also could have belonged to another Hospitaller nun," Anne replied. "Many come from high-ranking families."

"Keep the ring. Perhaps you can find a way to identify the owner without arousing suspicion."

"You trust me to proceed with much discretion."

"Have I not done so since I first came to Tyndal Priory?" Eleanor did not have to say more. In those early days of her leadership, she had allowed Sister Anne and her once-husband, Brother John, to meet in private, trusting that they would remain chaste.

"And I shall not disappoint you now."

Eleanor again looked longingly at the open window, and then resolved to remain content with a tiny glimpse of the sky. "I have some news that may please you. I have gotten permission for you to accompany the priory infirmarian, Sister Richolda, when she next visits Sister Amicia, as she must now be called."

Sister Anne grinned. "How fortunate that has been approved by her! When the infirmarian and I parted, she invited me to do just that, after we had a most interesting conversation in private."

Eleanor spun around. "Did she say if she had studied Mistress Hursel's corpse?"

"She is a most observant woman and grasped without asking that I was interested." Anne explained what Sister Richolda had told her about her findings after examining the corpse. She also relayed what the infirmarian had said about the priest and her own suspicions about why Sister Richolda might have chosen to convey the information gathered at the examination to her.

"Although it should not be difficult, Brother Thomas must find reason to become friendlier with this priest," Eleanor replied.

"Sadly, I did not have the time to pursue more details of the stabbing and certainly nothing about this ring."

"If you have another moment alone, you can ask her those questions."

"She carefully waited to talk to me until after Janeta left the room. I do not know why she felt the need for caution. Janeta is the former prioress' maid and serves her still. I came to no conclusion. Perhaps she did not want to be seen as gossiping about the servant's mistress."

Eleanor nodded but offered no opinion. "I have also learned sad news. Prioress Emelyne told me that Sister Amicia is suffering from a canker in her breast. She believes she is dying."

Anne gasped. "The infirmarian said she had become quite frail of late and suffered an illness, but she did not say what it was."

"If Sister Richolda is as wise as you suggest, she may welcome your opinion on this ailment. Whether this influenced her decision not to protest either accusation or condemnation is worthy of consideration, although I cannot imagine why it should. She will soon face God's judgment."

"Might she be protecting someone?"

"I, too, had considered that. But whom? I fear this problem grows more complex the more we learn."

"What do you wish me to do when I accompany Sister Richolda?"

"Observe all. Ask any question you feel you may without revealing your purpose. I cannot advise more because I cannot be there, but I trust your good judgment."

Anne bowed her head.

"And spend what time you will with the infirmarian on matters that you find useful for our hospital work as well. In the meantime, I will summon Brother Thomas. It is possible he has learned something important that we should know. Perhaps Janeta can take the message."

Sighing, the Prioress of Tyndal stared at the bed, knowing that Janeta would soon return and end her precious moment of freedom.

Once her prioress was safely tucked in, Anne opened the chamber door. As she stepped out, she saw Janeta approaching and told her that Prioress Eleanor wished to see her. Then she left to go to the chapel for prayer since she had missed one of the Offices usually honored at Tyndal.

The maid entered the room, with head down, and asked what she might do to serve.

Along with all the other puzzles, Eleanor found the maid to be a riddle. On one hand, Janeta behaved as if she expected to be struck at any moment. Yet she had displayed both sullenness and some arrogance earlier as well.

A thought to muse on later, she decided and then said, "I summon Brother Thomas to render his advice on a troubling spiritual matter. Please take the message to him immediately. I must speak with him as soon as possible."

"Yes, my lady," Janeta replied and left.

As the wooden door thudded shut, the silence in the room grew oppressive, and Eleanor began to understand how Amicia might feel, confined to a small cell when she once had had the freedom of a castle and then this priory, a place more open to the world than most religious houses.

"Yet she will soon enter the realm of eternity and stand before the terrible face and all-seeing eyes of God," she murmured. A shiver of dread coursed through her.

One day she must do the same.

Chapter Sixteen

Prioress Emelyne glowered at Janeta with a ferocity that the maid's news did not merit.

She was so weary, a state that often sparked a flare of temper, but, as she glanced at the stone floor around her, she realized it had grown less cluttered since the last Office. Seeing this progress extinguished the ember of rage that had threatened to blaze. Still, her eyes burned from straining to read far too long in the smoke from the candles.

"You must do as Prioress Eleanor has requested," she said. "Tomorrow morning just after the first Office."

Janeta kept her head bowed and hands clutched tightly against her waist.

Why must the woman tremble so? Emelyne found her behavior irritating, although she knew Janeta's uncertain future gave her cause. Yet she had never liked her and quickly dismissed interest in the maid's fears.

"Instead of seeking out Brother Thomas, however," she continued, "you must first tell Brother Damian that our honored guest wishes to see her monk. Then convey to my dear brother in kinship and faith that Prioress Eleanor seems to be in too much pain to endure such a meeting at present, but I will send word as soon as she is well enough. After delivering that message to my brother, return here forthwith. Brother Damian will speak to the monk."

Emelyne's lips twitched into a brief smile. If God were kind, this future message would include word that her troubling guest had healed and was eager to leave this priory.

"I shall obey, my lady."

Emelyne reached out for another charter.

Janeta hesitated.

"You have something more to say?"

"What shall I tell Prioress Eleanor if she asks why Brother Thomas has not come to do her biding? I fear she will."

"Indeed, she shall, as would I if I had been so cruelly confined with that painful injury." Emelyne slapped her hand sharply on the desk.

The maid flinched.

"You must say that he has been delayed and you do not know when he will come."

Now Janeta was sweating.

Sitting back, Emelyne felt a twinge of pity for this creature who had, for all her faults, been a loyal servant to the former prioress. "Fear not, child. If Prioress Eleanor insists on further explanation, tell her that I will respond to her if answers are, in truth, required."

Doubt remained on Janeta's face.

Emelyne took a deep breath. Must she tell this maid every word to speak? "And should she ask if you spoke directly to her monk, you may say, with no stain on your conscience, that you had first to seek permission from Brother Damian to do so. Such is only proper and is our practice. And further say that when he asked the purpose and you relayed the simple message, he told you that he would speak to Brother Thomas himself. I can assure you that he will say just what I have told you." She and her brother had always thought alike. She had full confidence that he would do what was required.

Bowing with courtesy, Janeta finally left, much to the prioress' relief.

Emelyne rose, went to warm her hands at the joyfully snapping fire, and tried to turn her thoughts to something more agreeable than irksome monastic guests.

Pets, she thought. Some prioresses have pets. Perhaps a small dog would bring her comfort when she was appointed permanently to this position. Glancing around, she decided a basket with a bit of old wool might go over in the corner near the door to her private chamber. Of course, she would not allow the beast to sleep with her. Somehow that seemed inappropriate if one were vowed to God. On the other hand, she might. She would pray about it.

With a sigh, she returned to her desk, stopping briefly to pick up a couple of rolled parchments from the floor.

Prioress Amicia had had a more masculine mind, Emelyne thought, one that retained figures and details as if a monk had carefully inscribed each thing in her head. The former leader had rarely needed to find the document to remember all the pertinent facts.

Emelyne did not have a similar facility. She had to read everything, refer back to sources, and file things in an order she could recall. Not that she doubted her ability to lead the priory in a profitable fashion, as was her duty, but her method could never be the same as that used by the woman locked in a nearby cell.

She set the rolls to one side and spread out the charter she had been reading before Janeta arrived. Immediately she began to rub her eyes. She had read so much, they began to hurt the moment she started reading again. What was this one about? A fine gift of thirteen acres of meadow plus eight acres of wood populated with deer!

Was the steward using this to the greatest benefit? Was he adequately competent, or did he let some things slip by his notice? Not only did she want to send more money to Clerkenwell for the efforts in Outremer, but she would like some needed repairs done for the benefit of the religious.

If only she had an advisor, she thought wearily. Brother Damian might aid her, but his first responsibility lay with his few monastics and the priest. If there was any question about use of resources, he would insist on his priorities superseding hers. They might have shared the same mother's womb, and most certainly were often of one mind, but he was still a brother and his word must rule.

Perhaps, once these Fontevraudine pests had left and she was confirmed in her position, she could consult with the former prioress. They had always had differences of opinion, but Sister Amicia was dying, and surely such trivial issues would no longer matter. Service to God was paramount to them both.

Emelyne turned away from the smoking candle and gazed at the stone walls around her. Why was she so uneasy? Wasn't she properly elected by the religious? And Amicia was dying. What difference did it make if her own elevation was now or after the former prioress' death?

Closing her eyes, they burned unbearably. She let the parchment roll up on itself, rose, and sought a cup of the mulled wine left for her comfort on the table beside the fire.

Chapter Seventeen

The canonical hour observed, Brother Thomas and the tiny band of Hospitallers emerged from the chapel.

Looking to the heavens, Thomas wondered if God wished to show His satisfaction with their orisons. The sky had lightened from an earlier dull grey to a recognizable blue. Sunlight actually spread across the courtyard with enough vigor that the men smiled, their eyes shining with pleasure.

But the monk had more important things on his mind than the weather. Out of the corner of his eye, he saw that Brother Martin had gone immediately to Brother Damian's side and was engaged in animated conversation.

The commander bent his head to listen, but his narrowed eyes betrayed impatience.

After their brief conversation the day before, Thomas might still think Brother Martin owned a certain innocence, but he held no such opinion of Damian. Forcing an expression of eager friendliness, Thomas approached the silent brother knight and the garrulous youth.

"May God grant our pleas," the monk said with noteworthy enthusiasm, "for the Office was well honored with sweet song and fervent prayer."

The two men jumped apart like lovers caught in a compromising position.

But Thomas doubted very much that they were. He knew the signs of plotting as well as the difference between guilty love and blameworthy deceit. With a broad grin, he waved at the sky as if suggesting God might send another sunbeam. In this case, he specifically longed for a light to shine on the crime he was trying to investigate.

Brother Damian recovered first. "We have brother knights and sergeants fighting in Outremer, Brother Thomas," he said without warmth. "That adds an even greater zeal to our humble devotions."

"I'm sure Prioress Eleanor would discover the same ardor in the preceptory if she were able to worship with the nuns." He waited.

Both men nodded, but there was an obvious hesitancy.

"Now that the Hour has been observed, I shall visit her." Thomas hoped his simulated heartiness was not too obvious.

Brother Martin blanched.

Not well-versed in deception, Thomas thought, but he was oddly pleased that the youth was not.

Brother Damian frowned. "I fear she may not be able to welcome you, Brother. Did I not hear that Prioress Eleanor's ankle was so badly injured she could not walk? If so, I doubt she prayed with the nuns and therefore must be confined to her chamber in the nuns' dormitory. Unless a nun is dying, not even a priest is allowed to visit therein."

Thomas knew he had made a mistake by suggesting his incapacitated prioress might attend the Office for prayer, but his shock that he was being denied the right to visit her was genuine.

Now he was worried. Prioress Eleanor would never deny him access to her unless she was afflicted with some vile plague. If conventions prohibited his visit in the nuns' quarters, she would find a way to be carried to where they could meet. Something felt amiss here, but he was not sure exactly how serious this attempt was to keep them apart. A chill struck him. Was she even safe?

"I knew she was in pain but did not know the full extent of the severity. She had not been thoroughly examined by Sister Anne before I was brought here. This news gravely concerns me, Brother Damian. I must speak with Sister Anne," Thomas replied. "She can relay any message our prioress has for me as well as explain the state of Prioress Eleanor's health. We do not wish to abuse your hospitality any longer than need be."

"I fear such a meeting with your sub-infirmarian will be difficult..."

"If Brother Martin accompanied me to meet with Sister Anne? I understand that a stranger, albeit a monk and counselor to Prioress Eleanor, might trouble the good nuns at Mynchen Buckland." He smiled with forced geniality at the aforementioned lad.

The lay brother greeted him with a blank expression and turned with a desperate look to his commander for guidance in how to respond.

Brother Damian ignored him.

Thomas countered the leader's intimidating frown with a gaze filled with a longing to accommodate. "Surely Prioress Emelyne would find no fault if Sister Anne came to the cloister where others often meet with Hospitaller nuns. With Brother Martin by my side and all of us in clear view of many others, there is no chance..."

"Brother Martin can relay any message to a nun or Prioress Emelyne that you might have and return with the reply. Why go at all, only to wait for a response in the garth, when you can stay here on your knees, praying to God for the swift recovery of your prioress?" Damian's grin was strained. "Surely, you would find that the most profitable activity."

Trying not to be insulted by the implication that he was less than devoted to the efficacy of prayer, Thomas replied to this suggestion with an expression of innocent puzzlement. "I am sure you did not know that I have often assisted Sister Anne at our priory hospital, conferring with her on treatment. Both she and our prioress would be perplexed if I did not offer advice in this matter."

He glanced first at Brother Martin, who bowed his head, and then at Brother Damian, who did not. "Indeed, it is my duty to do so, as I am sure you would now agree."

Brother Martin shifted from one foot to the other.

Thomas continued when Damian said nothing. "Yet I would not be the cause of any disquiet amongst the nuns," he said. "Surely the presence of Brother Martin, while Sister Anne and I conferred in the public area, would be adequate reassurance for them."

Brother Damian stared at Thomas.

Thomas failed to blink.

Damian clutched his scarred stump. "A wise solution, Brother," the commander quickly said.

Thomas wondered at the swift change. The man's eyes were glazed and his cheeks pale, as if he had just seen a frightening vision.

"Provide your greater wisdom to your sub-infirmarian so that your prioress' recovery may be swift. Although we have no wish for you to leave until she is able to travel, I know you all long to return to Tyndal Priory as soon as possible."

"Your Christian charity is exemplary in its kindness," Thomas replied, "and we do not wish to abuse it." He bowed. "If you will give Brother Martin permission, we will be on our way to the women's preceptory now and may thus return quickly."

Brother Martin's brow furrowed with worry.

Sweat had broken out on the commander's forehead. "I ask that you wait for only a short while longer to do so. Brother Martin has another duty he must perform for me first. When he is done, I will send him back to you. This task should not take long."

Thomas was not pleased, but he feared that further argument might not be wise. So he bowed his head and uttered his willingness to wait.

With an abrupt nod to the monk, Damian put his hand on Brother Martin's shoulder and firmly guided him in the required direction.

Thomas watched them depart. He did not resent being forced to accept the company of Brother Martin, a man who could easily be distracted and had not yet proven he was possessed of much sagacity. That was an easy enough problem to circumvent. What troubled him most was that the commander did not want him to communicate with Prioress Eleanor.

Somehow he must find a way to convey this strange plan to Sister Anne. How they could then find a way to freely communicate was a harder question to resolve.

Chapter Eighteen

Brother Damian slammed the door shut, grateful to see the back of Janeta the maid.

He had never liked the woman. In recent days, she bore herself with a feigned meekness because her mistress had been convicted of murder and was no longer prioress. In the past, she exuded an unnatural arrogance for a woman of her birth. Why Sister Amicia had tolerated her was beyond his comprehension.

But today this creature had accosted him in her old manner at his chamber door, demanding he listen to her message before he could obtain the relief he desperately sought. Had he not been in such agony, he would have shoved her to the ground where she ought, by all rights, to be groveling.

Another jagged pain cut into his upper arm from the stump below his elbow. Each time it felt like the blade that had sliced off his hand had struck him again. He could still see it arcing through the air with cruel precision, the sword flashing in the sun of Outremer like the weapon held by the angel at the gates of Eden. It was an image that often invaded his dreams and tore him screaming from sleep.

Groaning, he hastened to the table and grabbed the vial containing the pain-easing poppy juice. For just an instant, he glanced at the mazer he used to portion out his dosage but threw back his head, upended the vial, and drained the contents.

The easing warmth seeped through his body and even more swiftly dulled the pain from his old wound. Tears rolled down his cheeks. Slowly, he began to look on the world with greater ease. As for failing to adhere to the proper dose, he would tell Sister Richolda that he had spilled the bottle and must therefore beg for more.

The agony he suffered was the main reason he had insisted that Brother Thomas delay his visit to the preceptory by claiming Brother Martin had a task to perform. In fact, Damian could no longer bear this pain that often attacked without warning and seared its way from his stump into his shoulder. He had been in no state to decide the exact instructions he should give the youth. After his dose, he knew he could handle the problem of the monk's desired visit with greater ease.

When he and Brother Martin had arrived at Damian's chamber, he had ordered the lad to remain outside so he could take his medicine in private. As he opened his door, Janeta ran up to him, shouting that she had an urgent message from Prioress Emelyne. He had no choice but to take her into his audience chamber. So he might honor his vows, he kept the door partly open but ordered Brother Martin to stand further away so the message would not be overheard.

Since he had already told Brother Thomas that he could not speak with his injured prioress, he ordered the maid to tell his sister that all had been done in a satisfactory manner, then abruptly dismissed her with no further details. Emelyne would expect him to handle this wisely. He and his sister had always understood each other very well.

Sliding into his chair, he grew quite pleased with himself. Although his sister had used the excuse that the Prioress of Tyndal was in too much pain to see her monk, Damian decided he had been cleverer by claiming the meeting would be improper.

Because the primary work of the Hospitaller Order was charity done in the secular world, not enclosed contemplation like the Benedictines, questions were often asked about how strict the Order religious were in matters of chastity. To allow a monk to enter the nuns' dormitory would cause scandal.

He blinked. His chamber seemed to be slowly tilting at an odd angle. It was not an unpleasant sensation, but he decided to remain seated.

Suddenly, he raised his arms in delight. As much as he loved his sister, she could never have thought of this cunning plan! "Brother Martin!" He roared so the lad could hear him.

The young man looked around the partially opened door, his expression suggesting both fear and confusion.

"Stop staring like a dull-witted ass. Come in!"

Brother Martin edged into the room and softly closed the door.

"You will not accompany Brother Thomas to the preceptory. There were rats in the chapel today. Find a cat and set him on the hunt to destroy the vermin."

Looking oddly relieved, the youth bowed his head with respectful obedience and reached out for the door.

"I am not done with you."

Brother Martin stopped and instantly folded his hands with the proper humility.

"First, you must find Father Pasche and tell him to come to me immediately. Then seek the cat."

The youth did not move.

"Now!"

The young man fled, and Damian leaned back in his chair. It was just as well that Martin not be sent with Brother Thomas.

The lad owned a usefully pliable nature. Although his spirits had seemed low when he first arrived, Brother Martin was not prone to querulousness and disobedience like other youngest sons, forced to vows, and had never once slipped into the village to swyve willing women. Of late, he had actually grown more eager to spend time on his knees in the small chapel.

All that was commendable and the reason why Damian had chosen Martin to attach himself like a leech to the side of the Fontevraudine monk, but the youth was also simpleminded. He was not the one who should watch over Brother Thomas when he spoke with Sister Anne. Father Pasche was far better suited to what the commander now had in mind. In fact, he smiled, the priest was almost as clever as he.

Gazing up at the ceiling, he found the bracing of surprising complexity. Why had he never noticed this before? Pleasantly bemused, he became lost in contemplation of it.

Then he blinked, suddenly realizing that too much time had passed. Where was Pasche? Hadn't he sent for him a very long time ago?

A mild irritation began to infect his current serene mood, and he thumped his fingers on the arm of his chair. Had Brother Martin failed to promptly deliver the message? What other reason had Father Pasche for taking this long to obey his summons?

There was a knock at the door.

Damian roared permission to enter. The sound of his own voice hurt his ears, and he felt his face flush.

The priest stepped inside and shut the door behind him. "May God bring you blessings, my lord. How may I serve you?"

"You took long enough to obey my summons." Damian failed to mute his irritation, and a small voice inside his head reminded him that was rarely wise.

"I was hearing the confession of one of our lay brothers. You know the one who alternates between long periods of silence and extensive descriptions of his paltry sins? Even God must lose patience. When I saw Brother Martin arrive and indicate he must speak with me, I attempted to bring the recitation to an end, but stubbornness is one vice our dear brother never confesses but suffers in excess. I finally brought him to a halt by assigning some particularly lengthy penances. He left quite pleased."

Damian chuckled, his mood restored. "I have a task for you. Let me explain it quickly, for Brother Thomas awaits you." Then he confided to the priest far more of what was needed than he had planned to tell Brother Martin.

"I welcome the opportunity, my lord."

"I thought you might. Join Brother Thomas now. He has been long delayed and might be uneasy about our motives."

"I shall apologize profusely and be a pleasing companion to him." Pasche grinned.

With a brief instruction to also request another vial of poppy juice from the infirmarian to replace the one he had carelessly spilled, Damian sent the priest on his way.

After the chamber door closed, he rose, braced himself against the furniture and walls, and inched his way along until he reached it. Carefully, he looked outside.

No one was there.

"Good," he murmured, and then with an equally measured caution, the commander of the priory wove his way into his private room, collapsed on his narrow bed, and plunged into the depths of a dreamless sleep.

Chapter Nineteen

When Sister Anne saw the woven shirt, in which sharp thorns were entangled, that Amicia wore under her habit, she bit her tongue lest she gasp in horror. Many religious wore hair shirts that chafed the skin and were populated with colonies of fleas or lice, but this torment was beyond the practice of any she had known.

"I advised you to remove this, my lady," Sister Richolda said in a tone that would make a saint tremble.

Sister Amicia simply raised an eyebrow.

"I have brought you a clean habit, my lady," Janeta said, laying the clothing down on the bed. "Do you wish to change while I am here to help you?"

"I am no longer *my lady* but a loathsome sinner," Amicia replied with a nod to both women. "As for my thorn shirt, I shall wear it until I die. Even after my last breath, I must be buried in it and have told Father Pasche. When I donned this years ago, I did so as penance for those grave transgressions committed before I took vows. Now, of course, I have even greater need for it. It is my only hope to escape the fires of Hell."

"And it has caused wounds in your breasts and back that are no longer healing," the infirmarian retorted.

"I am dying, Sister Richolda. It matters not if such minor injuries putrefy."

Her shock subsiding, Sister Anne watched the infirmarian bathe the angry cuts with a concoction of water betony and took note. She might have used a wine cleansing followed by an application of honey. Later she would ask Sister Richolda to explain her choice. Perhaps water betony was more effective in certain situations?

But what could the former prioress have done to require such a horrible penance as a shirt of thorns even before the murder? She could think of no crime that would warrant such a thing and yet allow the sinner to live. Her curiosity growing, she decided to see if Amicia would tell her.

"I understand the world, Sister," Anne said to the former prioress. "Before I took vows, I was a wife and mother. There is much temptation outside our priory walls, and we all sin." The sympathy in her voice was genuine.

Amicia smiled in silent response, but her eyes revealed that she knew what this woman from Tyndal wanted to know. They also politely conveyed that she refused to give her what she wished.

With a brief nod, Sister Anne indicated that she understood and would not press the question. Instead, she turned to watch Sister Richolda prepare her draught of opium in wine.

"At least you are now willing to take this medicine," the infirmarian said, pouring a small amount into a cup and handing it to the former prioress. "For that small concession, I am grateful."

Drinking it with one swallow, Amicia grimaced and handed back the mazer. "It often helps me sleep without pain or dreams, and I pray upon awakening that Death will be that kind." She sighed. "Yet it will not, so I take the ease now. Eternity will be hard."

"Do you wish me to seek out Father Pasche, my lady?" Janeta's eyes were moist, but her tone was eager. "I have just returned from delivering a message to Brother Damian. The last Office has been completed, and it is not yet time for the next. The priest should be free to attend you if I leave now."

"That might be wise, child. Tell him I have nothing new to confess but that speaking with him might bring solace. I would be grateful for his company and wisdom."

The two nuns waited while Janeta quickly helped Amicia into her fresh robes. Sister Richolda winced when the former prioress settled the thorn shirt over her shoulders and newly treated wounds. One began to bleed again.

Then the three took their leave and left the cell.

Janeta hurried off to summon the priest. Anne and Richolda walked more slowly back to the infirmary.

"The draught I gave our former prioress was used in Outremer by both Jewish and Muslim physicians who sometimes helped with surgeries like amputations. It eased pain, according to one doctor, and he also claimed that patients survived the traumatic procedures in greater numbers with the opium. Although many Christians believe pain is meant to be suffered to the fullest as an acknowledgement of our sins, it seems the Muslims and Jews do not."

Anne laughed. "Not all Christians believe pain must be endured for the good of their souls either. My physician father did not."

"As I said earlier, your father was an exceptional man. I may believe in penance and rejection of the demands of the flesh, but I also believe God intended for us to show mercy. If suffering is obligatory, perhaps He is the best judge of when it must be endured and not mortal men." Richolda put a gentle hand on the nun's arm. "Do not repeat my words, Sister, for some might call them heresy."

"I swear myself to silence." Anne was surprised and pleased by the infirmarian's words as well as confidence. They also reminded her of the favor she wanted to ask. Reaching into the pouch at her waist, where she carried medicines at Tyndal, she pulled out the ring and showed it to Sister Richolda.

"I found this in the cloister garth and wish to return it to the owner. Do you recognize it?"

With a puzzled expression, Richolda fingered it for a moment. "I cannot be certain, but I believe I saw it once in Pri…Sister Amicia's possession." She looked up at Sister Anne for a long moment, then said, "I just remembered that I meant to bring her a salve to use on her wounds and must retrieve it from my apothecary shelf. Shall I take this ring and ask her if she recognizes it when I go back to her cell?"

Anne hesitated just long enough.

The infirmarian read her meaning well. "If it is hers, shall I return it to her if she desires? If it is not, but she knows to whom it belongs, do you wish me to give it back to you so you may tell the owner how you discovered it?" She looked at the ring with sorrow in her eyes, then back at her companion.

"I would be most grateful if you would do so, Sister," Anne replied.

Chapter Twenty

Father Pasche oozed charm.

It was much like a fishmonger touting rotten fish as a bargain, Thomas thought. Pasche's unsubtle attempts to flatter had also quickly grown stale. For one thing, Thomas did not think he would make a fine mentor to Brother Martin, nor had Brother Damian assigned the lad to be his leech in hopes that the Fontevraudine monk would.

"It must have been a terrible shock when the nuns' former prioress was convicted of murder," Thomas said. Perhaps the remark was too transparent and abrupt, but it was one anyone might make who had just learned of the events.

"It grieved us, but I confess the verdict was not a great surprise." The priest's tone was casual.

"How so?" Thomas suspected he had been meant to ask the question but was willing enough to comply.

"I have long known her. My elder brother was Sister Amicia's husband."

Thomas came to a sudden halt and stared at the priest. How many questions dare he ask the man in the short time before they entered the priory walls? "You had cause to believe she was capable of murder?"

The priest raised his hand in a cautionary gesture. "Rumors only, Brother, but, if repeated, one must consider whether they might not hold a grain of truth."

For the first time, Thomas suspected Father Pasche was not telling a lie. Yet he was wary. Facts can be shaded into deception just as lies can be made to sound like truth. "I have heard she refused to confess, yet also failed to claim innocence. Had she been accused before of some crime and behaved the same way?"

Pasche shook his head to suggest great reticence, then sighed as if forced to tell the tale. "She was suspected of murder once before but never tried. After my brother's death, it was whispered that she had pushed him down the stairs. No one formally accused her, but many thought it odd that he had fallen and broken his neck."

"And you?"

Pasche hesitated before replying, "I was in residence here as the priest at the time, but I, too, was surprised by the unexpected manner of his death." He looked at the monk and almost smiled. "If a woman kills her lord husband, surely she is capable of killing anyone. Has she not already invited the Devil on the path to her soul? I linked the past suspicion with her current refusal to deny her guilt and was convinced she had murdered Mistress Hursel."

The gate to the priory was open. An aged nun waited for the men to enter.

Thomas solemnly nodded, unable to respond otherwise to what the priest had just told him. How could he confirm that such a rumor about the death of Amicia's husband had even been bruited about? And if it had been, was it true? Might Prioress Eleanor have been cunningly deceived by a double murderer? It was equally possible that this priest had misled him by telling him a lie he was incapable of verifying.

At a loss for words or any plan of action, Thomas remained silent.

As the men walked into the courtyard, Father Pasche immediately called to a lay sister, telling her to bring Sister Anne to the cloister. Then he recalled his other charge and asked her to tell the infirmarian that Brother Damian had spilled the vial of medicine prepared for him and needed another.

Looking around him, Thomas suddenly felt a chill. He was too familiar with violent death to be uneasy at the scene of a murder, but the tale this priest had told about the convicted woman's husband put his humors out of balance. Melancholy began to wrap its icy hand around his heart and tint his reason with a heavy grey.

Fortunately, the sub-infirmarian arrived quickly. Thomas edged the despondency aside and greeted her with a tranquil mien.

"I know that Prioress Eleanor is in much pain yet unable to see me because she resides in the nuns' quarters," he said to Anne and turned his head slightly so he could give her a wink on the side the priest couldn't see.

Sister Anne did not betray him, confirmed his statement, and begged him to pray that God ease their prioress' suffering.

"As do we all at the commandery," Father Pasche added with appropriate gravity.

The monk bowed his gratitude. "The head of this commandery, Brother Damian, has been most kind in assigning Brother Martin to attend to my every need. His dedicated companionship has already made my stay most pleasant."

"And Prioress Emelyne has done the same for Prioress Eleanor. Janeta, the former prioress' maid, serves us with a most devoted charity." Sister Anne looked properly thankful.

Thomas noted that Father Pasche's smile was growing a little brittle.

So did Sister Anne. "I do have wonderful news, Brother," she said with marked enthusiasm. "Prioress Emelyne has given me permission to study the methods of the resident infirmarian, Sister Richolda, who learned much at the Order's hospital in Acre. I have visited her patients and accompanied her to treat the former prioress, Sister Amicia, who suffers from a great tumor in her breast." The sub-infirmarian nodded at the priest with a sorrowful expression and modestly lowered her eyes. "I am grateful for this opportunity, while Prioress Eleanor is unable to travel, to improve my knowledge of healing. Your Order, Father, is as highly respected for the charity of your hospitals as it is for the prowess of your brother knights in holy war."

Father Pasche seemed relieved and his features developed a more honest earnestness. "We are honored by Prioress Eleanor's visit but abhor the suffering she must endure from her injury. If we can provide a tiny gift of greater knowledge to your well-regarded hospital at Tyndal Priory, we are gratified."

Thomas loudly cleared his throat. "I do not wish to take up any more of your time, Sister. If you have the advice of Sister Richolda, perhaps we need not discuss the treatment of our prioress?"

"I always require your insights and wisdom, Brother," Anne said, indicating subtly that she understood his meaning.

They kept their discussion short but believable, then Thomas added, "Should Prioress Eleanor need my services, I am sure a messenger can be sent to Brother Damian who will know where I may be found."

The sound of someone running down the path startled the trio of monastics.

Janeta came to a halt in front of them, her face pale and her body reeking with sweat.

"Is all well with Prioress Eleanor, child?" Thomas looked at Anne and saw that she shared his fear.

"Yes, Brother!" the maid gasped. "Is there a message I could take to her?"

He glanced at Anne.

She raised an eyebrow to suggest she was equally puzzled.

"No message that I have not given to Sister Anne," he replied. Nor was there anything more either he or Sister Anne dared to say, so he added, "Perhaps you will convey to Prioress Emelyne that I beg the favor of her nuns' prayers so our prioress may have a swift recovery."

Something was troubling this woman, he thought, but he had no way of discovering the cause.

The priest glared at the maid and immediately suggested that he and Thomas return forthwith to the commandery.

"Father!" Janeta stared at him, her eyes round with some undefined emotion.

He waited with an impatient frown.

"Sister Amicia asked if you would go to her cell for she has need of your comfort."

"Is her wish an urgent one?"

Janet swallowed several times. "She did not say so, but I know her soul is troubled."

"Please tell her that I will come immediately after the next Office."

Thomas noted that the priest's expression had turned gentle. Could Father Pasche possibly grieve over the fate of a woman who might have killed his brother as well as Mistress Hursel? Yet he had seemed firm in his belief that she deserved her conviction. Such contradictions were always worth remembering and resolving, he thought.

He bowed to Sister Anne and nodded to the priest that he was ready to leave.

• • ● • •

As Sister Anne pretended to watch them depart, she kept one eye on Janeta. Either she is sick or profoundly agitated about something, the sub-infirmarian concluded. For a second time she found herself asking, "Are you unwell, child?"

Although it had seemed impossible, the maid turned even paler and the reek of her sweat grew stronger. "It is nothing now," Janeta replied in a tone that was less than convincing. "My mistress sent me to find Father Pasche, but I could not do so. I did not want to fail her!" Briefly, she put her hands over her eyes. "No one told me he had left with Brother Thomas. I did not know whether I should return here or continue to seek the priest."

Anne put a calming hand on the maid's arm. "All is well," she said in a soothing voice. "You made the right decision to come back, and you have done what your mistress required. As for Prioress Eleanor, I was with her, so you were not remiss in any obligation there. No one can claim that you did not do as you were commanded."

Janeta looked at her, then wiped the sweat from her face. "I ran all the way back here. Now I am just short of breath but will soon recover."

Anne was oddly unconvinced by this but had no valid reason to question the maid further.

Without another word, Janeta turned away and quickly left the garth.

The sub-infirmarian paused before leaving. The feeling that something was wrong extended far beyond Janeta, but she could not define it. Unfortunately, this reminded her again of the deadly illnesses of the abbots last winter. "Please let me not be so blind again in discovering the cause," she whispered to God.

As she walked back to the chamber she shared with her prioress, Sister Anne unconsciously felt in her pouch for the ring, now missing because Sister Richolda had possession.

It might well belong to the convicted woman, and that fact only added to the likelihood of Sister Amicia's guilt. Other than Sister Richolda's belief that the woman was too frail to stab Mistress Hursel, Anne had discovered little to suggest the former prioress was innocent. And even frailty was weak evidence, as the infirmarian had pointed out.

This is truly a hopeless task, Anne thought with sorrow. "If only this problem would just vanish," she prayed in a soft voice. "I want to return to our priory and heal the sick to the best of my ability in God's name. I am weary of violence and safely uttered lies."

Chapter Twenty-one

When the door to the priory slammed behind them, neither priest nor monk said anything further to each other as they walked the short distance back to the men's house.

The temporarily displaced gloom resettled like a sharp rock in Thomas' soul, and he felt no inclination to further joust wits with this priest. Yet he mulled over the information the man had given him and noted the priest's own pensive expression.

Perhaps Father Pasche regretted divulging as much as he had, or maybe he had simply grown weary with the effort to distract Thomas from seeking troubling facts. In any case, they shared a silence that was oddly companionable.

When they reached the door to the commandery, Father Pasche seemed to remember the need for courtesy to a guest, no matter how unwelcome, and he turned to the monk with a rigid smile.

But the door flew open, and an agitated lay brother burst out. "Father Pasche! Brother Thomas! You must go to the fishponds at once! Brother Martin has been found dead!"

The man's arms flapped about in consternation, and for a moment Thomas was reminded of a chick tentatively trying to fly.

But then the words sank in. "Brother Martin is dead?"

The priest glanced at Thomas with blatant incredulity, then back at the lay brother. "Both of us?"

Gasping, the man recovered his breath and nodded with an emphatic vigor. "Brother Damian requires you both."

Thomas returned the priest's look with an equal show of confusion. "We must go," he said.

With a wave of his hand for them to follow, the lay brother hurried off with Thomas close behind.

Father Pasche hesitated, then joined them.

• • ● • •

Brother Damian knelt by the lifeless body of the young religious and sobbed. When he heard the sound of the men approaching, he tried to mute his groans, but tears stubbornly continued to flow.

How ashen he is, Thomas thought. Despite the commander's past stern demeanor, the monk could tell that he truly grieved.

Rising to his feet, Damian ignored the priest but nodded to the monk and swiped at his cheeks in an unsuccessful effort to hide the evidence of his sorrow. "Thank you for coming so quickly, Brother," Damian said, and angrily rubbed again at the remaining dampness. "I need your expert opinion."

Thomas was surprised. How inconsistent, he thought. The commander must doubt the death was accidental, but why assign the dead man to shadow me and then ask me to examine the spy's corpse?

He bit back a sharp retort and instead replied with gentleness. "Perhaps Father Pasche should first whisper comfort into Brother Martin's ear while there is still time to give the peace of hope to his lingering soul."

The commander blinked as if he had forgotten the priest was even there. "Of course he should."

Keeping some distance from the dead man, Father Pasche stood motionless and stared at the body, his color as white as the corpse's face.

Thomas was puzzled by the man's reaction. This would not have been the first body the priest had ever seen, and probably not the first who had died by misadventure. He would have done the ritual himself, but he was not of this Order. Pasche was.

"Father Pasche?" Damian walked over to the man and put a firm hand on his arm. "His soul is in agony, and he did not deserve this fate."

The commander's touch startled the priest, and he stumbled backwards.

Damian grabbed him lest he fall, and then jerked the man forward. He gestured to the corpse with his stump. "Now!"

With incredible slowness, Father Pasche approached the dead body, collapsed to his knees, and began whispering into the dead lad's ear.

Thomas watched him with astonishment, then felt the hot breath of someone standing too close.

"Brother Thomas, I beg a favor of you," Brother Damian muttered. "Please examine our brother's body and tell me if this was murder."

Thomas bent over the dead youth and studied him. Martin's head was wet, and his robes were drenched from his shoulders to waist. "Where was he found?" he asked, looking up at the three assembled Hospitallers.

Father Pasche now stood many feet away from the others and stared into the tall grass toward one willow tree near the pond bank.

The lay brother who had led them here pointed to the fish-pond. "I found him lying over there."

"Show me."

The lay brother took him to the spot. "He was lying in the water, almost up to his waist. I pulled him out by his feet, but, as soon as I laid him down on the path, I knew he was dead." Pushing a fist to his mouth, he tried to stifle a sob. "I went immediately to tell Brother Damian."

"And for what reason had you come here?"

Damian had overheard and replied, "I sent him to seek Brother Martin. Earlier, I had ordered the lad to find a cat to hunt the rats in the chapel. When he never returned, I wondered why."

Thomas glanced back to the trembling lay brother. "Show me what you did after you pulled him out."

"It was here that I made sure he was not breathing." He pointed to the spot on the path. "And then I took him by his feet and dragged him this way." The man gestured as he walked to the place where the body now lay. "It was easier than lifting him…" He seemed embarrassed as if he had insulted, or even hurt, the dead boy by dragging him.

"Was there any reason why you put the body there?"

The lay brother bowed his head. "The grass looked soft and dry," he murmured. "I thought he would be more comfortable." Grasping the incongruity of what he had just said, he began to weep.

"That was kind of you," Thomas replied and gripped the man's shoulder in sympathy. Then he walked carefully around the area. The mud in the path was so thick it would never hold the imprint of a foot, he thought. Then he gazed at the edges of the pond, but all he could see was where the earth had crumbled. This could have occurred if Brother Martin had slipped and fallen in or when the lay brother had pulled him out. Now there was no way to tell if it had been intact before the lad had drowned.

Yet if the earth collapses under a man, he will usually go into the water feet-first, he thought. If he is pushed, he is more likely to fall head-first. If he slips, however, he could fall either way. Perhaps the loss of this particular evidence was irrelevant.

He could see the heavy weeds floating in the dark water. Were someone to fall head-first, he might have become entangled in them and unable to pull himself out. The mud would not allow purchase by feet or a desperate hand. And he noted the torn weeds where the lay brother said he had pulled the body out.

Except for one fact, he might have reasonably concluded that the evidence suggested a tragic accident. That detail was the depth of the water. Although that might have risen far higher elsewhere, he doubted the depth here was greater than a couple of feet. To have drowned in so little water, the youth was either unconscious or terrified.

Thomas turned toward the Hospitallers. "Could Brother Martin swim?" If he could, he would have been less likely to have panicked when he fell in.

Pasche did not raise his eyes. "No," he replied in a barely audible voice.

Thomas turned back to examine the drag marks through the grass leading back to the body. He wasn't certain, because the lay brother had been somewhat imprecise about the route he had taken after pulling the body out of the pond, but he saw spots in the nearby grass that might have been trampled down quite recently. The heavy rain had ceased and would not be the cause. In other places, slightly further away, the grass was unbroken. Trying not to step into the areas, he tried to peer around for any evidence but found nothing.

"Why would he have come here if he was searching for a cat?" The lay brother shrugged.

Brother Damian scowled. "I have no knowledge of cats."

"They sometimes come to eat dead fish," the priest replied.

Thomas went back and knelt again by the side of the body. If the lad had seemed innocent in life, he looked almost angelic in death—or would have, if his eyes were not staring as if he had just seen Satan. Gently, the monk ran his hands over the boy's lids to close them.

With sadness, he studied Brother Martin's face. It was filthy with mud and littered with strands of pond weeds. There were a few scratches. Not deep. Any blood would have been washed away. But they could have been the result of pulling him over pebbles and bits of wood in the bank if he had been lying facedown.

He sat back, then asked the lay brother, "Was he lying facedown or faceup when you found him in the pond?"

"Down," the man said, and gulped uncomfortably.

Then the scratches were most likely the result of dragging him out of the pond and onto the path. Next, Thomas felt the chest, shoulders, and arms but found no broken bones. There were no tears in his robe that would suggest stabbing, and his neck was without mark. Strangling was not the reason the man had died.

The monk next looked at the fingers and nails. They were free of mud. "Were his hands in the water?"

"I don't recall," the man said.

The hands were damp, so Thomas assumed the water might have washed them clean, destroying any evidence that the lad had struggled to gain purchase on the slippery bank. Sitting back, he regretted he did not have a private place to more thoroughly examine the naked corpse and also wished Sister Anne was beside him with her greater knowledge.

Very gently, he turned the body over and felt the back of the head. As he did, he found the evidence he feared. The back of the youth's skull had been shattered. The wound would have been fatal and could not have occurred in this soft earth by accident.

Brother Martin did not drown. He had been murdered.

He swallowed a groan and quickly gazed around but knew his wish had no hope of being granted. Any rock or other implement would have been tossed somewhere into the pond.

The commander was instantly by his side with the priest close behind. "Is all well, Brother?"

Thomas made a swift decision he feared he might regret later, but he had no cause to trust either of these men. With one questionable death already and the strange decision to keep him from speaking with his prioress, he didn't know how the news of another murder would be greeted. Standing up, he brushed his hands free of dirt. "The most likely conclusion is that poor Brother Martin died by accident."

When Father Pasche exhaled an audible sigh of relief, and Brother Damian shot the priest a warning look, Thomas concluded that his choice to lie might have been the right one.

Chapter Twenty-two

Sister Anne finished telling her prioress about her odd meeting with Brother Thomas in the cloister.

"If he has been assigned a guardian, then we have one as well," Eleanor said. "Janeta is clearly our watchdog."

"I know nothing about Brother Martin, but I sense that the maid does her assigned duty with some reluctance," Anne replied.

The window to the outside was firmly shuttered, and Eleanor glared at it once as she paced. Her impatience was palpable, and her frown was more eloquent than any words. Abruptly, she stopped. "What is your opinion of the lass?"

"She seems genuinely devoted to Sister Amicia," Anne said immediately, then stopped to think. "But her future is in doubt."

"I asked her about what she might do when her mistress can no longer keep her in service. She replied that God would decide. A worthy conclusion, but He has given us latitude to find our own paths. I wonder if she has thought about that, and, if so, what she has concluded." Eleanor resumed her pacing.

"I have never noticed her laugh, yet rarely has she been sullen while assigned to us. If serving us is not pleasing to her, she has never been less than obedient."

"Any unhappiness is probably due to her uncertainty about her near future. But do you trust her?" Eleanor stopped and waited for her friend to think about this.

The answer was almost immediate. "No."

"Neither do I."

"We are in agreement that she is not the one we might entrust to take Brother Thomas a message?" Briefly, the sub-infirmarian smiled.

"Not unless we wanted it to pass through Prioress Emelyne's ears or eyes first, for she must be the one who assigned Janeta to watch us."

"So there is a deliberate plan to keep Brother Thomas from communicating with us, and we are equally denied contact with him. Why? Do they not believe you injured your ankle and that is the sole reason we have remained here longer than planned?"

Eleanor sighed. "Either my artifice was believed or it doesn't matter. We do enjoy some reputation in solving crimes, and that can make those suffering guilty consciences grow uneasy if we remain near them too long."

"You suspect either or both Prioress Emelyne and Brother Damian killed Mistress Hursel?" Anne was shocked.

"I cannot say that, but they must have some purpose in keeping us apart and assigning us guards."

"If they killed Mistress Hursel, they are dangerous, and our own lives may be in peril."

"Even if Prioress Emelyne or Brother Damian were involved in the death of Mistress Hursel, why would Prioress Emelyne harm us and endanger her current position? If two or more murders were to occur now at Mynchen Buckland, the Prior of England would swiftly send a delegation to investigate the calamity." She touched her friend's arm. "I think we might have some confidence in our safety."

Anne shivered. "I would rather we not be the cause for such an investigation by Clerkenwell."

Eleanor agreed. "Nor do I have any intention of letting such a thing happen. Our ability to find the actual killer is limited, even if we had the right to freely question people here. Our best hope is to prove that Sister Amicia cannot be guilty, or even that the crime should be more thoroughly investigated before she receives a final sentence. I fear we can do little more."

"And thus you could keep your word to the former prioress. Will it allow us to leave here unharmed?"

"Sister Amicia is dying. Had the murder not occurred, it is likely, from what you have learned, that Prioress Emelyne would have been chosen after her death by the nuns to lead them. Why would she want to harm us if all we do is convince her that her former leader is innocent or likely so?" She tilted her head and watched her friend, then added, "And why would the new prioress want to kill Mistress Hursel and make sure Prioress Amicia is found guilty if her eventual election was so certain? It is unlikely that she had any doubt in the matter. Election results are rarely a surprise."

Anne looked at Eleanor for a long time before asking, "You don't want to uncover the murderer?" Her tone revealed her skepticism.

"Of course I do! But we must be prepared for a lesser conclusion to our search." Eleanor sat down on the bed. "To make sure none of us becomes the next victim of this murderer, we might consider whether or not we should allow Prioress Emelyne and her brother to understand that our only wish is to show that Sister Amicia is highly unlikely to have committed the crime."

"You would take the woman into your confidence?"

"Only if required. It is always wise to plan for more than one road to the destination lest one is blocked."

"Since it is clear that we cannot speak with Brother Thomas, nor he with us, what other path can we take?" Anne threw up her hands in frustration.

"You have said that Sister Richolda is trustworthy?"

Anne nodded.

"She is the only infirmarian here. That means she provides salves and potions to the men's house. If she does, and is willing, we might ask her to take a message to Brother Thomas with her next basket of herbs. Perhaps there is a way she can set up a meeting between you and him?"

Chapter Twenty-three

Father Pasche sipped his wine, but his sour expression suggested he found little pleasure in it.

Brother Damian slammed his cup down on the table. "What is troubling you?"

"Why did you ask the monk to examine the corpse? Do you trust him or not? And if you do, why bother asking me to act as a barrier to any communication with his prioress? I am not the king's fool and here only to amuse you, Damian."

"You do not have the sense of a king's fool! Do you not realize there is a murderer out there?"

Pasche's hand trembled, and a splash of wine dampened his black robe. "What do you mean?"

"We thought the former prioress killed Mistress Hursel. Now Brother Martin is dead. The killer is still free."

Pasche stared at him. "Brother Thomas said the death was an accident."

"The monk lied."

"If so, and I have my doubts about that, then we urged the conviction of an innocent woman?" The priest's face was ashen.

Damian shrugged.

"This is no casual matter! It was you, not I, who first insisted Prioress Amicia killed the woman. It was you who said she had cause to murder her because of dark secrets in her past. *Dark secrets.* Your words, not mine."

"I did not say she had, only that we might as well accept a guilty verdict. Why contest the accusation when there was no proof anyone else did it, she was the most likely suspect, and she is dying anyway? We all agreed to beg the Prior of England for a merciful incarceration here since her death was imminent."

"Et cetera! Et cetera!"

Damian leapt to his feet. "Do not mock me, Priest!"

"Sit down, Commander. There is no ridicule in my words, only anger. You tell a twisted tale of our discussion that night, and now I suspect you have lied to me for your own secret reasons. Perhaps you have done so for some time now."

"Lie?" It was Damian's time to grow pale.

"The evidence against her was weak. How could a dying woman thrust a blade into another with such force? Why not assume she had simply found the body and her hands were bloodied from handling the corpse? As for not mentioning Prioress Amicia's dark secrets, you most certainly did!"

"It is you who have chosen to forget our discussion. Perhaps," he said, looking at the cup in the priest's hand, "you had drunk too much of my wine that evening. Shall I remind you of what was actually said?"

Pasche glared. "If I did drink more than is my custom, I was not alone," he muttered. "Yes, do continue with your version of the facts."

"Remember when I asked if you never suspected that the manner of your brother's death was questionable?" Damian was shouting. "We both concluded she had committed the crime because she has killed before!"

"The story was that he was stinking of wine. He was drunk. He fell down the stone stairs." Pasche swallowed the rest of his wine and put the cup down. "You did not say she had killed before but did ask me that question, and then suggested she had *dark secrets*." With a sneer, he glanced at the commander, then at the ewer of wine, and poured another cup.

"I did not speak in some language you do not know. I assumed you understood my meaning. You admitted you had always wondered why he fell that night, as opposed to other drunken nights when she was not present."

"There were rumors. Yes, I wondered. But she is a woman, tall but never possessed of unnatural strength for her sex. My brother was a soldier, a knight…"

"Now it is you who lie. At the Chapter trial, you did not defend her as a weak woman, incapable of thrusting a knife into the heart. You reminded all that Satan could have given her the strength."

Pasche pressed a finger to his temple as if pondering a complex religious mystery. "Was it your voice or the Devil's I heard as I argued that?"

"Your own! Dare you now attempt to say that you did not think further on it, after you had heard the news of his death, and realize that your brother had been killed by his wife? You admitted your suspicions!"

Pasche fell silent, drained his cup, and poured himself more. "I confess that I did when we talked of it after Mistress Hursel's death because you tempted me with Satan's voice. Now that I have recovered my reason, I doubt that she could have done so. The Devil would have had to have sent ten of his imps to give her hands the necessary power. My brother was a huge man." His voice was hoarse.

"He was drunk, staggering. You'd seen him after he had too much wine. A child could push him over."

Pasche looked at him in amazement. "You sound as if you had been there."

"Mistress Hursel told me that Sister Amicia pushed him down the stairs," Damian roared.

The priest laughed but his face was pale. "Did Mistress Hursel see the crime? Or was the butcher's widow so dear to my sister-in-law that they chattered together like little girls, holding hands? Servant and mistress? Did my sister-in-law confess to the crime with a giggle or with a tear?"

Damian grunted. "She never told me exactly how she knew, only that she did. Those were the dark secrets of which I spoke, and you understood exactly what I meant."

For a long moment, the priest studied the commander. His pallor had faded, but his eyes were now narrowed in anger. "Why did you think this woman was telling the truth?"

Damian waved his hand in vague circles. "Details. I have since forgotten them, but, at the time, they convinced me."

"And why tell you? Why not take her tale to the sheriff?" Pasche put down his cup and folded his arms.

"She knew the dead husband and I had fought together in Outremer. It was he who saved my life when…" He looked at his stump.

The priest hesitated as if waiting for the commander to say more, and then he said, "I ask again. Why not go to the sheriff? A woman who kills her husband is hanged or even burned at the stake. A husband is like the king, monarch of the family. This is treason. And were you not angry that your friend, the man who had saved your life, and my brother, had been murdered?"

"Would you have wanted the scandal?" Damian whispered.

"Now I must conclude that she told you because she wanted something to stay quiet." The priest's voice was low as if talking to himself.

"A small gift of money. The woman's own husband had just died and left her a pauper." The commander's voice had also dropped.

"I think there was more to it than that."

Damian shrugged. "She was a collector of secrets. She led me to believe there was much more she could tell that would bring shame on your family." He now slammed his fist on the table. "God's blood, Pasche! I was protecting you and your kin! Is that a sin? And I continue to believe that a woman who killed her husband was perfectly capable of killing the woman who knew her secret." He sat back in the chair and glared. "And you concurred when we spoke together that night."

"Let us return to the issue at hand!" The priest's voice shifted to a growl. "Brother Thomas has declared that Brother Martin's death was an accident. Why do you insist there is a murderer still free and suggest it is the same one who killed Mistress Hursel?"

"Because I think the monk lied. I now think the person who killed Mistress Hursel must have killed Brother Martin. Even Egypt was not cursed with a plague of murderers when the pharaoh denied the Israelites their freedom. Why would we suffer far worse than they?" He banged his fist. "There is one killer!"

The priest turned scarlet. "You think. You *think*!" he shouted. "You base your conclusion that my sister-in-law killed my brother on the word of a woman of questionable veracity whose primary motive in telling you her tale was extortion. You assume a monk of some reputation is lying when he says our brother died accidentally. I have had enough of your *thinking*, Damian."

Damian's face was scarlet in the pale light. "Conclude what you will, Father Pasche. I am going to see Prioress Emelyne since she must know of this death." With that, he pushed the priest aside and escaped down the hall.

Father Pasche put a hand against the wall to steady himself, turned to the ewer of wine and poured another large cup.

He swiftly drained it.

Chapter Twenty-four

"Brother Martin is dead?" Prioress Emelyne stared at Damian in horror.

Her brother explained the circumstances of his discovery, where the body had been found, and then added, "Brother Thomas and Father Pasche were returning from your preceptory. I called on the monk to inspect the body."

With an incredulous look, Emelyne sat back in her chair. "Please explain, dearest brother, why we are keeping the Prioress of Tyndal and her clever monk apart, lest they grow unnecessarily curious about Mistress Hursel's death, if you have chosen to involve Brother Thomas in your lay brother's death?" Her smile suggested more than a hint of mockery.

"It is inappropriate for your infirmarian to touch the body of a man vowed to God."

"Was there any doubt that he was dead?"

Damian glared. "That question is unworthy of my reply."

"Your first response was feeble. Perhaps your second will be better. So I ask again. Why? Was there any reason to think a violent misadventure had occurred?"

He bowed his head and said nothing.

Prioress Emelyne jumped up and shook her brother by the shoulders. "You have fought in Outremer! You know the signs of violent death better than most physicians. Why not examine the corpse yourself, if you feared a crime had been committed?"

"I could not trust my judgment in the matter."

"You need not tell me. You wept like a woman when you saw his corpse." Her acid tone oozed contempt.

He stiffened. "I do not like your implication. There was nothing sinful in my affection for the lad. You knew him. He was a dullard but had a pious and virginal heart."

"Nor did my words mean what you suggest." She stood back with hands on her hips. "I have known women with sterner resolve than you usually own. As a boy, you wept when you skinned your knee."

His face scarlet with rage, he picked up the empty candlestick from her desk and hurled it against the wall. "How dare an inadequate creature, made from the rib of Adam, question my courage and determination?"

A nun opened the door and peeked in.

Emelyne waved her away, then bent to pick up the cracked candlestick. "The cost of your fit of temper will come out of the next allotment planned for your maintenance projects." She gestured for him to sit.

He remained on his feet, breathing like an asthmatic dragon.

"Let us discuss this problem with greater calmness. Arguing with each other is not wise until the ankle of our nemesis has healed and the party of Tyndal monastics has left us in peace. We must resolve any misunderstanding without the use of verbal trebuchets." Glancing at the candlestick still in her hand, she placed it on the table. "Or the use of my few possessions as a substitute for a boulder."

He sat down. "Bring me a cup of wine."

She did as he bade. "I remind you that we share our father's sinful choler, and warn you that mine is as ready to flare as yours. So, as a start to our reasoned conversation, I shall begin with the news Janeta brought me. Brother Thomas and Father Pasche were in our garth, talking to Sister Anne. I had thought you would tell the monk he could not visit because his prioress was in too much pain."

"He was prepared for such a simplistic excuse," Damian growled. "He argued that he must confer with Sister Anne about

Prioress Eleanor's health. She would expect him to do so, as he often does at their priory. I concluded that we must allow them to continue their reasonable practice, as it would be unnatural if they did not. For all her reputation, Sister Anne is still a woman and needs the guidance of a man in her work."

Emelyne's face glowed pink, and she bit her lip as he spoke. Then in a steady voice she replied, "I agree."

He smirked. "Although I had already assigned Brother Martin to watch over the monk, I decided that Father Pasche was the wiser choice to accompany Brother Thomas to your preceptory. His wits are swift enough to deflect any problems, and he was willing to assist. I planned to learn all the details of the meeting later."

His sister nodded with greater approval. "Another wise choice. And what did occur in my cloister garth? Janeta arrived too late to tell me many details of their conversation."

Damian spent a moment flexing his only hand as if it pained him.

Knowing her brother's methods of delaying response, Emelyne closed her eyes and swallowed twice to avoid shouting at him.

"Nothing of interest," he replied. Then he dropped all pretense of a painful hand. "I have since found cause to wonder about our priest."

Surprised at his change of tone and subject, his sister tilted her head to indicate he had her full attention.

"When he saw the lad's corpse, he was visibly upset. That did not trouble me, as any man who had known Brother Martin would feel the same." He glowered at his sister, but the look was brief and perfunctory. "The youth lay on the ground, his soul still hovering nearby in fear and longing, and no one was offering the hope of God's mercy. It was Brother Thomas who suggested the priest whisper comfort in the youth's ear. Father Pasche should have done so without being reminded and has performed the ritual before."

Leaning forward with interest, Emelyne nodded.

"When we retreated to my chamber, he began to drink heavily, as he has been wont to do in recent days, and expressed doubt over my decision to let the monk examine the dead body."

Emelyne lowered her head. This was not the time to remind him that she had just done the same and therefore had no quarrel with the priest.

"After some discussion, I told him that I believed Brother Martin had been murdered by the same person who killed Mistress Hursel. He was visibly shaken."

As he might well be, Emelyne thought, for I am, as well. But she had sworn not to argue so chose courtesy and said, "Before you continue, I beg a response to two questions. Did Brother Thomas do a thorough examination of the corpse? What was his verdict?"

"He was thorough. He said the death appeared to be accidental."

"Then why…?"

"Because the monk lies!"

"If you did not trust him, I see absolutely no reason to have him inspect the body." This time there was an edge to her voice.

Damian leaned toward her with a smug grin. "Because I wanted to know whether he would give me the truth or a lie."

"And thus you confirmed that the monk is as devious as we had already suspected." Emelyne tried unsuccessfully to rid her voice of fury.

His face grew red.

"Have you considered that we may have overreacted to the arrival of these particular monastics, Brother, and thus caused them to wonder about events here more than they would otherwise have done?"

He did not respond, and his color remained fiery.

"Prioress Eleanor has injured herself on the uneven stone floor. She is forced to remain in bed for a few days until it heals. According to Janeta, she expresses frequent dissatisfaction with her state and grows impatient to return to her priory. Her sub-infirmarian suffers ill-health but wants to learn from Sister

Richolda about her experiences in Acre. What is either unreasonable or suspicious in all that? You said yourself that Brother Thomas should be expected to consult with Sister Anne about their prioress' ankle. When you sent Father Pasche with him, did the monk protest?"

"I confess he did not. Initially, he even suggested Brother Martin accompany him." Suddenly, he put his hand to his eyes and muttered, "And I now wish I had done so!"

Emelyne offered no solace.

Wiping his eyes, he continued. "The Tyndal monk seemed willing to be governed by our practices."

"And now you believe that the monk lied about the nature of Brother Martin's death and that proves he plots against us? I see no basis for suspecting it. Our former prioress continues to accept her guilt, or so Janeta has told me." Opening her hands in appeal, she said, "Explain to me why we continue to worry about Prioress Eleanor and her monk wanting to delve into a crime they have no cause or authority to investigate?"

"You agreed to exercise caution with these monastics. They have the reputation of being overly curious about things they should not." He looked pleadingly at his sister.

Emelyne recognized the expression as his concession to her logic and decided to be satisfied with a silent victory. "And I still do, Brother. There is no reason why the verdict should be questioned and confirmed by the Prior of England. I only wished to point out that we may have taken our caution too far. Perhaps it is enough to rely on Janeta's reports to me. It will not be long before Prioress Eleanor has healed and leaves us."

Damian nodded but remained grim. "Then we are in agreement, Sister, but we have another problem to consider, as I was about to explain before you interrupted me with questions about the Fontevraudine religious."

"Please continue." Despite their disagreements, she felt a chill when she heard the concern in his voice.

"I do believe that the monk either lied to me about Brother Martin's death, or he was less thorough than I assumed he would be." He nodded with courtesy to his sister as if kindly conceding she may have been partially right. "But Father Pasche's behavior at the fishponds and his later manner in my chambers, when we discussed the boy's death, are still disconcerting. His reactions might be innocent, but there is another factor that casts doubt on that."

Now curious, she urged him to continue.

"I did think Prioress Amicia killed Mistress Hursel, and she may still be guilty, but now I have qualms. Father Pasche had grounds to kill Mistress Hursel himself and cast blame on your former prioress." He gestured a plea not to interrupt. "And, if he did so, he may have killed Brother Martin for a reason I have yet to fully uncover."

Emelyne opened her mouth in shock.

For once, her brother showed no inclination to gloat.

Chapter Twenty-five

Sister Anne and Sister Richolda had been explaining their preferred treatments of various ailments to each other with increasing enthusiasm.

Janeta was now fast asleep on the bench against the wall of the apothecary.

The infirmarian nodded in the maid's direction to her companion.

Anne looked over her shoulder, and the pair drew closer.

"The ring you found belongs to our former prioress," Richolda whispered. "According to her, it was a gift from someone dear to her and she used to keep it with her at all times, although she never wore it after she took vows."

"Does she know how she lost it?" Anne was disappointed with the news but not surprised.

"When I asked, she smiled in that perceptive way she has. We often saw it when she was not taken in by our petty evasions." Growing sad, Richolda continued. "She always was observant, and I failed this time to disguise my purpose for inquiring. She knew I was not asking for myself and merely shook her head when I tried to find a way to question her further. So I did not try and returned the ring to her."

"I had hoped for a different response."

Richolda touched her companion's arm. "So did I."

A loud snort from Janeta made Anne turn around, but the

maid seemed to be in a deep sleep. Not willing to take any chance of being overheard, however, she bent closer to Richolda's ear. "Do you believe she is innocent or guilty? Tell me the truth."

The infirmarian rubbed a finger under one eye. "My logic quarrels with my heart. The latter says *innocent*. When I discovered her shirt of thorns, I realized she was deeply repentant over some crime she, or her former priest, had deemed a terrible sin before she took vows. While she ruled us, she was a wise leader, compassionate but firm. Her humors always remained in balance. No prioress is ever universally loved, even those who are later recognized as saints, but no one ever claimed she was unfair or inconsistent. Is this a woman who is likely to murder another?"

"Did she have any cause to kill Mistress Hursel?"

Richolda shrugged and straightened as if her back pained her. "I do not know details and did not know our prioress before she arrived at Mynchen Buckland. At the trial, she said that she had known Mistress Hursel years ago and they had argued, although she claimed it was over a small thing. The relationship had been one of servant and mistress. If Prioress Amicia had sent her away for some infraction, any resentment should have been in Mistress Hursel's heart, not that of our prioress."

Anne noticed that the infirmarian had reverted to calling the convicted woman by her previous title. "What do you know of Mistress Hursel?"

"Little enough. She was the local butcher's wife. She may have come here on occasion, but I cannot swear to it. One nun, who had taken food to a poor family in the village, mentioned that the woman was known as a shrew, and some said she would cast her own child into the fires of Hell if it served some purpose for her. But that was stated by the husband of the poor family. When his wife fell ill, he took a few hours to care for her until others could assist. He was told he no longer had a job with the butcher as a result and later heard that the man's wife had ordered it."

The sub-infirmarian blinked. "Might a villager have killed Mistress Hursel in the priory garth?"

Sister Richolda shook her head. "Some may have wished to do so, but why would any commit the crime here when it would have been far simpler to do so in the village? Besides, there was very little time between when Mistress Hursel arrived and Prioress Amicia went to the cloister."

Anne nodded, then glanced again at the sleeping maid.

Janeta seemed to be stirring.

Gesturing for the infirmarian to lean closer, Anne quickly whispered, "I have a favor to ask of you."

"As I am able, I am willing."

"You take medicines or other healing items to the brothers' house?"

"Frequently. Most often to the commander who continues to suffer from pain in his mutilated arm."

"Shall you go there soon?"

"Today."

"Will you take a message to Brother Thomas for me?" She looked at the sleeping maid once more. "Only he can know of it."

Richolda grinned and nodded.

"I must meet with him tonight. Somewhere private."

"I will tell him where and lead you there myself."

"May God take your soul directly to Heaven for this kindness!"

"Your prayer humbles me, but I hope the need does not come too soon," the infirmarian said with a twinkle and then lifted her head. Her eyes said clearly enough that their time for private conversation had ended.

Janeta yawned.

Richolda took a deep breath. "And then the young mother in Acre turned with a look of great love at the small cot we had put beside her and asked that I give her the sweet babe who lay there…"

Chapter Twenty-six

Brother Martin's body lay in front of the small altar. Candles cast wavering shadows on his face, and his body gave off a whiff of rot. For those so inclined, it was a reminder that all living must return to the earth from whence they came. To those who had loved the dead man, it opened the heart to a flood of bitter pain, no matter how deep their faith.

Brother Damian knelt and wept. Had others been in the chapel, they might have heard brief snatches of incomprehensible prayer. His sorrow was evident and profound.

While often abrupt with the lad, he had cared for him. Brother Martin reminded him of a cherub in his innocence, a beautiful boy with no malice. And although the lad had never been a problem, always dutiful in the practices of faith, he had grown sweetly pious of late, spending hours praying in the chapel. On the very day of his death, he had glowed with a special joy after early communal prayer as if God had granted him some favor.

It was a state of purity the commander envied, although only Damian knew just how far from such virtue he was himself. Had it not been blasphemy, he would have said that penance was useless, he would never be cleansed, and even God could never forgive all his transgressions.

Brother Martin, on the other hand, had surely gone straight to Heaven.

He moaned, not from the pain in his old wound but in his

soul. No amount of poppy juice from a skilled infirmarian could cure that, and no priest ever had.

Gazing up, he stared at the corpse. The shadows mocked him, playing with the eyes of the dead man and making them appear to move.

Damian shivered. It was his fault that the lad had died, and now the youth's spirit was aware of it. "I shall make amends," he whispered, begging Brother Martin not to haunt him, and then he bent until his head struck the stone floor.

This was a pain he welcomed.

"The monk lied," he hissed to the stones. "This was neither an accident nor the result of the lad taking his own life. This was murder by another hand." He was convinced Brother Thomas knew it and had a malicious reason for not telling him the truth.

He suspected his sister was right. They had erred in so rigorously trying to keep the Tyndal monastics from looking into the former prioress' conviction, and it was his fault they had made that decision.

He banged his head again against the floor.

Only one still living knew he had cause to kill Mistress Hursel, and he had done all he could so no one would give credence to that testimony. Lest his secrets be revealed, however, he did not want anyone growing curious and asking careful questions about Amicia's conviction.

But it was now evident to him that the vile woman had been killed by someone other than Prioress Amicia. His willingness to let her take the blame because it was convenient, added to her own odd decision not to defend herself, had likely resulted in the death of the innocent boy. His corpse now lay before Damian as a fresh reminder of his darkening sins.

He had no regrets over the death of Mistress Hursel, only relief. She was a whore and earned her keep from her collection of secrets. After she learned how he had lost his hand in Outremer, she had mocked him for his cowardice and exacted a price for her silence.

She had often lain with Prioress Amicia's husband in ways no virtuous woman would. The man might have been Damian's friend, but his sins were profound. One night, when he had drunk too deeply, he told Hursel that Damian had fled combat and cowered in a nearby crevice. When he found Damian after the battle, he told him that he could either face the punishment for cowardice, a shame from which his entire family would never recover, or suffer a private penance and be sent home with honor. Damian chose the latter, not knowing what was meant.

It took but a moment. His friend told him to stretch forth his right arm, then drew a sword and struck off his lower arm just above his hand. After a rough treatment to stop the bleeding, he lifted Damian onto his horse and swiftly took him to the tent run by the Hospitallers near the battlefield. His friend told the brothers he had found Damian badly wounded in a crevice where he had crawled to die. A surgeon tended the wound and sent Damian to the hospital in Acre until he healed. Many months later, he was sent back to England and assigned to lead the commandery near his sister.

Mistress Hursel had threatened to tell the true story to the Prior of England if Damian did not pay her a fine fortune. And he did, embezzling money from the rents which were meant to help fund the hospital in Acre and the brother knights who fought the infidels.

When she married the butcher, she told Damian he need not continue the payments for she had a good roof over her head and food for her belly. Perhaps he should have been grateful, even wondering at her strange definition of integrity, but she now knew the source of the funds he used to pay her. That would be fodder for the next time she needed money.

When she had arrived at the preceptory and was murdered, he feared she had come to extort from him again. But now he was free of her, indeed of all who knew his shame. His spirit enjoyed the same relief from the woman's death that poppy juice gave the pain in his wounded arm.

And so he had had cause to rejoice over his newfound peace. The arrival of the party from Tyndal Priory and the subsequent injury suffered by Prioress Eleanor was a threat to that. He became fiercely determined to protect himself.

But he had not counted on this second death. After fleeing the battlefield in Outremer, he had committed other acts of cowardice, but this most recent had turned out to be his most despicable.

Mistress Hursel's enemies were surely legion, and he presumed that her killer, if it truly was not Prioress Amicia, would escape. Had he been the man, he would have fled as far as he could from Mynchen Buckland. Apparently, the murderer had not.

Did the youth see something he should not have seen that implicated one person in the murder? Had he been killed for that? And he would still be alive if Damian had not been so terrified that Prioress Eleanor and Brother Thomas might communicate with each other that he chose Father Pasche instead of Brother Martin to accompany the cursed monk from Tyndal.

Damian whined like a sick child and again beat his head repeatedly against the stones until his forehead bled. Then he lay flat and wept again, his cheek lying in his own shed blood. What must his penance be?

He knew well enough and begged God to take the bitter cup from him. Must he accept that his own sins would be discovered and that he would suffer the shame and consequences? Must he now humble himself and beg Brother Thomas to find the man who had killed an innocent boy?

He sat up, wiped the seeping wound in his forehead, and clenched his fist.

Was the murderer Father Pasche?

There had been a very long delay between the time Damian had sent Brother Martin to summon the priest and Father Pasche's arrival.

Who else could it be?

Chapter Twenty-seven

Sister Anne waited within the curtained branches of the willow tree close to the fishponds. It was near dusk, and Sister Richolda had warned her that there would be little time to talk before darkness made the walk back a dangerous one. The infirmarian could not wait, lest she be missed, nor did she want to know what the two monastics discussed.

Through the increasing shadows, Anne saw two shapes approaching and held her breath.

Brother Thomas pushed aside the branches and entered the meeting place. The other shadow turned and hurried back to her infirmary.

"I have heard rumors…"

Thomas interrupted her. "Brother Martin has been murdered."

Anne stifled a cry.

"He was found not far from here, head down in the fishpond. Although I did not see the original position of the corpse, I was told that his head and neck were tangled in the weeds. It appeared he had fallen in headfirst. All assumed he had struggled to get out but the mud was too soft to gain a firm hold while he was upside down, then the weeds wrapped around his head, he panicked, and drowned."

"You said *murdered*."

"Weeds could not have crushed the back of his head, and he had fallen in a shallow part of the pond. Unless he was unconscious, he could have gotten out. There was no evidence that he hit his head falling into the pond. No sharp rocks. He must have been dead before his body was dragged to the edge of the pond and pushed in. The weeds float about, which would explain why some were tangled around his neck."

"How did you come to know this?"

"When Father Pasche and I were returning from that visit with you in the cloister, a lay brother waylaid us, informed us of the death and Brother Damian's plea that we both come to the fishponds where the body lay. Once there, the commander asked me to examine the corpse."

Considering how much effort had been put forth to keep prioress and monk from talking to each other, Anne could not believe this. "Why would he ask you to do so?"

"I do not know."

"What did you tell him?"

"I lied and said the death was an accident."

"Why not tell him the truth?" Anne assumed Brother Thomas knew what he was doing, but nothing was making any sense and she voiced her confusion.

"I do not trust the man. It was he who assigned Brother Martin to stay with me like a leech and, most likely, report every word and movement I made. As for the killer, I do not know who that is, but if we conclude that the former prioress is innocent, then it may be the same person who killed Mistress Hursel. Perhaps Brother Martin witnessed something he should not have, and the lad might not have understood the significance of what he saw. Certainly, he appeared remarkably ignorant of worldly things, although I have known men who portrayed themselves as such to hide their cunning..."

"To set a spy on you but then ask you to inspect the corpse of the same man is most curious." She thought for a moment. "Might Brother Damian have killed the boy and then asked you to examine the body? In so doing, he might have hoped you would assume his innocence of the crime. How many murderers ask for a knowledgeable examination of the person they just killed?"

"Curious, indeed, but he seemed truly shocked and grieved." Brother Thomas started, as if he had heard a sound, but then continued. "But Father Pasche did act strangely. He looked very pale and avoided the corpse. For a priest, that was most unusual. He must have seen violent death before, yet I had to urge him to comfort the dead boy's soul, something he should have done the instant he saw the body. With great reluctance, he finally did but only after Brother Damian shouted at him to do so."

"Might he have feared that the corpse would bleed if he touched it and thus proclaim him the murderer?"

"That is quite possible," he replied. "Now that I think more on it, I recall that he very carefully did not lay even a finger on the corpse."

"What will you do?"

He shook his head. "I am not sure, other than try to watch him carefully, lest he betray himself by some other means. But tell me what news you have. Maybe that will show us the next road to take."

Anne told him about the ring she had found behind the bench where Mistress Hursel was killed. "Prioress Eleanor and I decided to trust Sister Richolda and ask her to show the ring to Sister Amicia for identification. The former prioress confirmed it was hers, but she could not say, or refused to do so, when she might have lost it."

"Which tells nothing about the guilt or innocence of the former prioress."

Anne quickly summarized what the infirmarian had told her about the position of the wound and her conclusions from that, as well as her doubts that Sister Amicia was strong enough to have killed the woman. "The former prioress is dying of a canker," Anne said. "I accompanied Sister Richolda when she visited Sister Amicia to provide palliative treatment. It is clear from many signs that the canker has driven its poisonous fingers deep into her. She has little time left to live."

"And thus the conclusion that she was too frail to kill Mistress Hursel seems reasonable."

Anne nodded. "She also wears a shirt entwined with thorns, which she donned long before this crime was committed. The torment would shame many a martyred saint. I do not why she suffers this hard penance. Although I tried to ask, she suspected my intent and refused to speak further."

"I wonder if that old sin would provide any clue to the current crime."

"She holds a few secrets in her heart, Brother. She has not yet adequately explained why she refused to defend herself. Oh, she gave an answer, but neither our prioress nor I believed it."

Quickly they shared what little else each needed to know, then Anne said, "It is likely that Janeta, the former prioress' maid, has been sent to watch Prioress Eleanor and me by Prioress Emelyne, just as Brother Martin was ordered to shadow you. Now that the lay brother is dead, do you think you will be assigned another leech?"

He shook his head. "There are too few at the men's house to do so. One is already watching the cell of the former prioress, and I doubt Brother Damian would try himself. He must suspect I do not trust him and that I have lied about the cause of Brother Martin's death."

"Who do you think is the killer, or are you convinced it is Father Pasche?"

"Apart from my current suspicions about the priest, the obvious suspects would be Brother Damian and Prioress Emelyne. They are the ones who worried enough about our presence that they assigned spies. Because of the force of the blow required to break Brother Martin's skull, I would assume the killer was a man and that would eliminate Prioress Emelyne. Yet the commander was profoundly grieved over the death of the youth. Do you know how Prioress Emelyne reacted?"

Anne shook her head. "I assume she has been told, but I do not know and thus could not observe any reaction."

Thomas looked around and realized the darkness was descending too quickly. "We must trust Prioress Eleanor to piece together the information we have shared and see if she can come to better conclusions. Both of us must leave now before it is too dark to see the safe path away from the ponds."

"It is possible we can meet again," Sister Anne said as they slipped out of their hiding place. "Janeta can be avoided, as she was tonight, and Sister Richolda is trustworthy."

"Then she can bring me a message."

They hurried as carefully as they could along the muddy path and soon found where it met the road between the two houses.

Sister Anne rushed back to the nuns' preceptory.

Thomas hesitated outside the brothers' house, inexplicably reluctant to return to his small cell.

Looking up, he noted that the moon was waning. From someone he had heard the story of a pagan goddess and her moons. If he recalled the tale correctly, a waning crescent meant a time of reversal when one might also make amends for malice done.

He shivered. This was a pagan tale, he reminded himself, but he could not help wondering if something was about to happen to reverse the darkness of the evil residing here and bring justice.

As he walked through the door of the commandery, deeply repentant for giving so much credence to pagan beliefs, he failed to notice that someone was watching him from the shadows of the chapel.

Chapter Twenty-eight

In the early morning hours, just after she had privately observed the early Office, Eleanor stood as close to the edge of the window as she dared and peeked outside.

The sun was struggling to rise, tinting the sky red at the edge of the earth and painting clouds in bruised purple while everything to the west remained dark blue. The prioress was uncertain whether this was God's way of relaying hope or His warning that it would be a day filled with grief.

Janeta had not yet arrived, nor had Sister Anne returned from prayer. Her sub-infirmarian would be horrified that Eleanor was risking exposure. But this enforced seclusion was becoming increasingly arduous. This was their fourth day here, and there was so little time left to accomplish anything on behalf of the dying woman Eleanor continued to believe was innocent.

Gazing down into the courtyard, she saw little activity. A nun, assumed to be the cellarer, was talking to a merchant who was gesturing with enthusiasm toward his covered cart. Eleanor smiled at the nun's lack of fervor over the man's attempt to get the highest price for his offerings. A good cellarer would counter with the reminder that less coin in exchange for God's blessing was of greater value to the soul. In the end, the two would come to a fair and very worldly price.

The shadows were quickly retreating and surrendering all but the deeper corners of the courtyard to God's light.

From outside her range of vision, the steward appeared. He must have come early to discuss the day's priorities with Prioress Emelyne, Eleanor thought. He was now walking purposefully toward the gate, and she wished she could see his face. Although he was reputed to be a cheerful and dutiful man, he had not worked long under the direction of this new prioress. Change meant the rebuilding of trust for them both, and, once again, Eleanor was grateful she had had Prior Andrew for many years to assist her.

Father Pasche, walking beside Prioress Emelyne, now came into view. Just below the window, they stopped, and he bent to speak more privately with the new prioress. His back was to Eleanor, but, in the glow of the brighter morning, she could see Emelyne's face. Was it the stiff breeze or had he said something to bring such high color to her cheeks?

The prioress glanced up, and Eleanor jumped back. Had she been swift enough to avoid being seen?

There was a knock at the door, and Eleanor rushed back to bed, settling herself under the warm blanket before giving permission to enter.

Sister Anne walked in and firmly closed the door. "At last we are able to talk. I have much to tell you," she said.

•　●　●　●　•

Eleanor sat on the side of the bed. "Who killed Brother Martin and why?"

"Brother Thomas does not know. He thinks that if Sister Amicia is innocent, the one who killed Mistress Hursel must have killed the lay brother as well. If she is not, there are two killers, yet that does not seem reasonable." Anne shook her head in frustration. "He doubts it was Prioress Emelyne since the blow to the youth's head took some strength, as did the stabbing of the butcher's widow. Brother Damian is possible but seemed deeply grieved over the boy's death. That leaves Father Pasche, and, as I mentioned, he behaved most oddly in his hesitancy to administer a priest's basic duty to the hovering soul."

"I wonder if corpses do bleed when murderers touch them." Anne thought for a moment. "I have known bodies to burst open if left unburied too long, and many do believe that corpses will bleed when their killer dares to touch them. Yet I have never had occasion to witness such a thing. Perhaps it matters only that many believe the tale to be true."

"I usually look for the simplest answer. Since Sister Amicia is dying and far too frail to have stabbed the victim, my confidence grows that she is innocent. Why she chose not to defend herself is another question and, I fear, has muddied the primary issue of guilt. For that reason, I set her refusal to claim innocence aside for the moment."

"The ring was hers."

"How and when it was lost near the bench remain questions, but the location neither proves nor disproves her guilt."

"So the murderer of one is most likely the killer of the other?"

"Yes, and the manner in which Brother Thomas and I have been deterred from speaking together leads me to conclude that the perpetrator is someone within this compound of commandery and preceptory." She fell silent for a moment. "Although some might say an angry villager could have slipped in and murdered the woman, I doubt it. The time between the arrival of the victim and the discovery of her death is too short. The possibility of being seen approaching the priory and going into the garth is too great...."

"Sister Richolda thought the same."

Eleanor smiled. "I am delighted to have that wise woman's concurrence."

"Brother Thomas hoped you would know far better than he who is the likely killer."

"I would not dismiss Brother Damian because he wept over the body of the young man. Killing someone who is loved in a moment of rage is no reason not to weep over the body when Satan has released his hold on the killer."

"And Father Pasche's reaction when he saw the body?"

"That perplexes me. I lack enough detail, and I fear we have missed something crucial. Why, for example, is everyone complicit in allowing the former prioress to take the guilt of this crime upon herself? Might the killer be someone we haven't considered? The steward, for instance? Was he here? Or…"

Someone knocked loudly on the door.

Eleanor leapt into bed. "That is not Janeta," she whispered to Anne before calling permission to enter.

Prioress Emelyne strode into the room like a storm-driven thundercloud. Her eyes were narrowed in fury.

Trailing behind was a ghostly pale Janeta.

"How dare you!" The Hospitaller prioress gripped her hands as if fearing what they might do in her rage.

Raising an eyebrow, Eleanor said nothing, her demeanor cold as ice.

"What plots are you hatching behind my back? I have done nothing to deserve this. Did I not offer you adequate hospitality when you were injured? Have I not sent Janeta to assist you? Did I…?"

Eleanor raised a hand. "If you will explain how I have offended you, we might be able to discuss this matter without undue recriminations."

"You are spying on us! Why?"

"And what has led you to make this accusation?"

Sister Anne poured a mazer of wine and offered it to Emelyne. The woman glared at the cup.

Eleanor wondered if the heat of the woman's gaze might boil the proffered wine.

But with a surprising shift to composure, Emelyne accepted the extended refreshment. "Your monk and this nun met in secret last night near the fishponds." She flipped her hand in the sub-infirmarian's direction. "Either you are spying on us or your two religious are breaking their vows of chastity." Her voice retained a sharp edge.

Sister Anne spun around and walked back to the ewer, covering her mouth with her hand. To anyone who did not know her, the gesture might have suggested guilt. To those who did, it would be clear she was struggling not to laugh.

Eleanor tilted her head and widened her eyes with an expression of mild surprise. "Most certainly I can assure you that Brother Thomas and Sister Anne were not engaged in lustful acts. In fact, we were discussing their meeting before you arrived."

"Then why were they sneaking around at night, under the trees, and near the fishponds?"

With a great sigh, Eleanor bowed her head. "Although you have generously sent Janeta to assist my sub-infirmarian with my care, and Brother Damian was sufficiently worried about Brother Thomas' safety to assign a man to accompany him at all times, there are occasions when I deem it advisable for my two monastics to speak together, although preferably in my presence."

Emelyne's forbidding scowl wavered ever so slightly.

Eleanor smiled gently at the self-effacing maid. "Of course, I am deeply appreciative of the attendants you have assigned to us." She bent her head with evident embarrassment. "Yet I have the right to keep some matters of health a private issue between those who treat and myself. Now it seems I must reveal this to defend us from unjust accusations." She glanced up at Emelyne with a look that could be interpreted as either mild anger or surprise at the need to explain herself.

Emelyne stepped back and opened her mouth to speak.

Eleanor waved her hand to dismiss the attempt. "I have some concerns that ought not, for purposes of modesty, be discussed in the presence of Father Pasche or Brother Martin. Although I have heard the sad news of the young lay brother's death, and shall pray for his soul, I believe that Father Pasche's ears would blush to hear of my womanly concerns."

The prioress' expression hardened. "Yet Brother Thomas may speak of such things without question?"

"Indeed, he can! At our priory, we send Brother Thomas into the village with medicines to treat those unable to come to our hospital. When he does this, he must sometimes help women who suffer from spreading sores in the womb or the painful teats of nursing mothers. Never once has he touched them or broken his vows in any way. The villagers call him *saintly.* Sister Anne and I have learned to rely on his advice."

Now standing away from the view of Prioress Emelyne and Janeta, Sister Anne watched her own prioress with increasing amazement.

"Thus he has some expertise in medical matters, unlike Father Pasche." Emelyne bent her head, speaking softly as if alone.

Eleanor did not respond.

The prioress abruptly looked up. "Yet why at night and at the fishponds?"

"Where else could they meet privately without Father Pasche joining them?" Eleanor shrugged. "Brother Thomas saw Sister Richolda delivering medicines to the commandery and begged her to tell Sister Anne to meet him after the mid-afternoon prayer at that place. There they might discuss the health issue to which I have just alluded. An acceptable request, wouldn't you say? And your infirmarian owns no fault in relaying the message..." Eleanor gave Emelyne a significant glance. "...unless she was ordered to disobey my reasonable desire for communication between two religious under my authority."

"She was not." But Emelyne's color had risen once more.

"As for the hour, it was not yet dark, although Sister Anne has confessed to me that their consultation lasted longer than either had expected. All this has been confessed to me. Both Brother Thomas and she have begged my forgiveness, which I have granted. The meeting may have been ill-advised, Prioress, but I know my monastics well. I am confident that their transgression was carelessness, committed out of desire to achieve a higher purpose of charity, not sin."

Knowing she dare not criticize the Prioress of Tyndal for her decision on her own two monastics, Emelyne said nothing but her eyes glowed again with fury.

"I hope you and I can come to a compromise in this matter so there will no longer be the chance for misunderstanding." Eleanor gestured to her nun to refill the woman's mazer.

Eleanor had noted that Janeta remained behind Prioress Emelyne without speaking the entire time, but now the maid gave off a foul stink. Even her robe was splotched with her nervous sweat.

Emelyne did not reply until she had drunk some of the wine. Now appearing calmer, she said, "I have no wish to quarrel with you."

"I propose that Sister Anne and Brother Thomas meet as needed without hindrance. Now that the soul of Brother Martin lies with God, I ask that your brother not assign another attendant to Brother Thomas on those occasions when my two monastics wish to speak about matters of no concern to the men of the commandery."

Emelyne's forehead creased with displeasure.

"Instead, I beg you to send only Janeta with Sister Anne so there will be proper attendance when she speaks with my monk."

The sub-infirmarian's mouth briefly opened and instantly shut.

Janeta's head snapped up. She did not attempt to hide her surprise.

Emelyne slowly smiled, this time with apparent relief. "I grant your plea, Prioress Eleanor. Your suggestion is a wise one." She looked behind her at the maid, then back at her guest. "And you may call on her to do so, no matter what time of the day or night."

"I am most grateful," Eleanor said, beaming in return. "There will not be any further meetings at dusk, however. Sister Anne and I have agreed that it was imprudent to do so last night."

"We are in amicable agreement," Emelyne said, and, after a brief exchange of meaningless pleasantries, left the chamber. At her command, Janeta followed.

• ● ● ● •

Anne rushed over to Eleanor and sat on the bed so they could whisper.

"I managed all that without lying too much," the prioress said. "The closest I came was the suggestion about my health problem, but solving this murder would give me much relief." Eleanor pressed a hand to her breast. "I wasn't sure I could succeed with the trick."

Anne laughed softly. "Well, we did agree that meeting by the willow tree near the swollen fishponds at dusk was dangerous and ought not to be repeated."

"Most certainly ill-advised!"

"Had God given you a man's shape, you would have made a fine counselor to the king! Never have I heard tales of anyone, past or present, who could obfuscate meaning as skillfully as you did this day!"

"Yet to further hide our purpose, I was forced to agree that Janeta might remain an observer." Eleanor fell silent as if she had heard a sound outside.

Anne listened, but then shook her head and bent closer.

"How well do you know French?" Eleanor asked.

"I learned enough, before I took vows, in our former apothecary shop to communicate with those merchants who came from there."

"Brother Thomas knows the language well. When you need to speak of secret things in the presence of our faithful maid, do your best with French and let us pray that Janeta is totally ignorant of the tongue."

"As I am ignorant of Latin," Anne said with a hint of sadness.

Eleanor squeezed her friend's hand. "We shall take our chances," she said, "but for the first time, I feel hopeful."

Chapter Twenty-nine

Sister Anne took her time walking the path to the commandery. The sun warmed the earth, and the air was filled with a fertile scent that promised new life. Her spirits rose. It was the first time, since the death of the abbots, that she had not been burdened with melancholy. Had she been a child, or even a young woman, she might have allowed herself to skip, but Janeta was with her.

I must maintain my dignity, she said to herself with amusement, and refused to hold back a sigh of contentment.

But then she turned and realized that Janeta was walking very slowly some distance behind as if she did not want to arrive at their destination.

The sub-infirmarian waited for her and, once again, noted how downcast the maid looked. Of course, the woman most certainly had cause. Her mistress was condemned as a murderer. Prioress Emelyne had presumably chosen her to spy on them because Janeta was the most vulnerable in the community. Being neither lay sister nor otherwise securely bound to the priory like the steward was, she had no assured place here. She might not have wanted to report to her prioress on all we said or did, but she had little choice in obeying and must feel very much alone. How lonely she must be, Anne decided, for the maid seemed to have no friend at all in the priory.

Yet there was no reason to believe Prioress Emelyne would not take her in as a lay sister or even a secular servant after her mistress died. The Hospitallers were known for their charity to the poor, and Janeta did qualify as that.

In the distance, a bird sang. It would soon be time for nesting and eggs. With the dark chill of winter, many men and women would have found warmth in each other's arms, and the sight of rounded bellies would become more common in a little while as well.

After darkness, light shines, Sister Anne thought, and death precedes eternal life. The seasons might teach God's lessons well, but she was now beginning to worry if her stock of medicines at Tyndal Priory was ready for the needs of birthing mothers. Sister Oliva was a treasure of competence, but Anne longed to be home.

Janeta was now standing quietly next to the nun.

"You all must grieve over the death of Brother Martin," Sister Anne said.

Janeta turned her eyes to the ground.

"Did you know him?"

"Everyone did," the maid replied.

"Did he have a special responsibility in the commandery? I know nothing of the practices of this Order in England, and there are so few men in residence here. I assume each bore a greater burden of duties as a result."

"He provided fish from the ponds for meals."

Sister Anne looked surprised. "He was a fine fisherman then! Did he use nets or a line?" This might explain why he was at the fishponds. Either he was fishing or he knew cats might come there for food. Yet she could not see how it explained why he was killed.

Janeta shrugged.

"Did he learn the skill from his father or did someone teach him here?" She wasn't sure the answer would reveal anything of value, but she was trying to be both subtle and probing while she was able to at least briefly question the maid.

"Father Pasche taught him."

Now that was interesting, the sub-infirmarian thought. Might it explain the priest's odd reaction to the boy's death? "Then Brother Martin did not grow up near a river or lake?"

Again, the maid shrugged.

She could not be less forthcoming if she were a rock, Anne thought with mild impatience. "Boys love to fish," she said, ignoring the sharp pain in her heart at the memory of her dead son proudly presenting her with a fish he had caught, albeit with much assistance from his father. "He must have enjoyed the lessons with Father Pasche."

Janeta looked at the nun with a flash of anger. "He was no boy, and he learned because it was his duty to do so."

Anne blinked at the unexpectedly sharp retort. "To a woman of my age," she said, "many men seem like boys, even when they have married and have sons of their own. I did not mean that he had not taken on a man's responsibilities in his vocation."

Nodding abruptly, the maid lowered her head. "I repeat only what Father Pasche said in my hearing," she muttered. "I should not have told you. It was said to my mistress, not me."

"I do not fault you," Anne said. The maid showed an admirable loyalty to the former prioress, she thought, then doggedly pursued her questions. She had managed to pry one bit of information from the woman. "So Brother Martin did not like fishing but considered it one of his many duties in serving his community and God."

"He liked to fish. I meant that Father Pasche never called him a boy."

"If the priest loved to fish and taught the skill to the young man, he must have been fond of Brother Martin."

"Why ask these questions of me?" Janeta suddenly shook her fists like a frustrated and angry child. Her face, however, was an unhealthy white. "I do not know the answers. I am not of this Order. I am a servant who tries only to obey the orders given to my by my mistress or Prioress Emelyne!"

Anne put a calming hand on the woman's shoulder. "I meant no ill, Janeta. My sin was idle curiosity and nothing more. It is a weakness, especially among women, and I shall seek penance for it."

The maid nodded, lowered her head once again, and fell into her usual silence.

As she had several times before, Sister Anne wondered if the woman was ill. Certainly, she often looked pale, or even green, and had seemed to suffer from nausea. But if she suffered this way just before her courses began, why did she not seek aid from Sister Richolda?

Then the sub-infirmarian began to study Janeta with a more thorough healer's eye, and a thought crossed her mind.

Might the woman be pregnant?

Chapter Thirty

The meeting with Sister Anne had been brief, and Brother Thomas watched the two women walk back to the preceptory.

He did not want to return to his cell, nor did he have any desire to kneel at the altar. The day was too beautiful and surely there was prayer enough in finding joy in God's creation.

Hesitating a moment, he turned to the path that led to the fishponds. He did not intend to reexamine the site where Brother Martin had died, but he needed time to think over what Sister Anne had just said about the priest and the lad.

Since Janeta had been there, the nun's news had been carefully phrased to express sorrow that the fish meals might be fewer now that the man who caught them was dead, although his fellow fisherman, Father Pasche, remained. She had turned to the maid and remarked that the man who had trained the lay brother would be hard-pressed to make up for the catch the two of them were able to bring to the monastic tables.

Janeta had said nothing while studying the ground with her accustomed intensity.

As he walked along the path, casually passing his hand through the tall grass, he wondered what the relationship was between Father Pasche and Brother Martin. He was equally curious about Brother Damian, a man who seemed calculated and hard of heart yet had wept over the lad's corpse. Although Brother Martin owned the innocent mien of a young boy and the soft features of a woman, Thomas had observed enough of him to conclude that, while he might have been inexperienced, he was not an utter child.

Did either or both of these men lust after him? Were they rivals for his affections? Did this explain the priest's hesitancy to look at the corpse? Was jealousy cause for murder, making the link between this and Mistress Hursel's death nonexistent?

The sound of a snapping twig made Thomas spin around. "Who is there?" he called out.

The soft breeze ruffled the tall grass like a woman running fingers through her hair. The air smelled of fresh sweetness. Only the buzzing of insects and birdsong answered him.

But Thomas was uneasy. Someone was watching him, but he saw no direct evidence. A person might hide in the grass, he thought, but he had seen no one follow him. It would be a long way from the compound of the religious for a man to crawl on his belly. He decided he was being foolish, walked on, and continued his musing.

Were he to guess, based on very little proof, he would conclude that the commander and priest both loved the youth, but he doubted either allowed himself to acknowledge overt lust for the lay brother. There may have been a rivalry between them for his allegiance, however. As Thomas knew, the boundary between the desire to bond lovingly and the passion to own, or even the line between love and lust, could be fragile or ill-defined. These were questions that he and Durant had debated on the few occasions they now met.

In the case of Brother Martin's murder, had the rivalry, no matter how tense, been enough for one man to kill the beloved? He thought it more likely that one of the rivals would have killed the other if passions rose that high. And yet...

Something that did not belong in the grass moved.

Out of the corner of his eye, Thomas spied a spot of dark color. That is not an animal, he thought.

Keeping his eyes down as if deep in thought, he stood very still and waited.

A man sneezed.

Twice.

Thomas gave up the pretense and waded into the grass. "Why have you been following me, Father Pasche?" he said, staring down at the priest.

• ● ● ● •

The two men sat together in a small area off the narrow path where the grass was beaten down. If they were not exactly friendly, they were at least courteous.

The priest rubbed at his nose and scowled. "The ponds stink of rot."

"You have not answered my question, Father."

"Who is spying on whom?" Pasche snarled. "Why can you not just leave us in peace?"

"Because I smell something more rotten than pond weeds here, and the more you avoid my questions, the closer to me the stench grows."

"The Devil is mocking you. There is nothing amiss here." The priest reached out to smooth the grass around him.

"Mistress Hursel's death. Let us begin there."

"A woman whom no one mourns! Why trouble yourself over that? None of us killed her, yet none of us condemns the person who did."

"Not one of you is guilty?" Thomas was incredulous. "Yet Prioress Amicia was convicted of the crime on evidence that any man of reason would ridicule."

Father Pasche swallowed and looked like he longed for a large cup of wine.

"I know she refused to defend herself, but she also did not confess to the crime. I have now learned she is dying." Thomas reached over and gripped his companion's shoulder. "Was she like the ram that conveniently appeared to Abraham and took his son's place as the burnt offering? Whose place did she take? Or was she merely the useful sacrifice?"

Shaking himself loose from the monk's grasp, Pasche hid his face in his hands and whimpered.

"I concede that her refusal to defend herself is puzzling," Thomas said, "but did it not occur to you that she might have had grounds to do this strange thing, yet did not kill the woman?"

"Brother Damian has finally confirmed that Sister Amicia killed her husband, my brother, and a man with whom our commander fought in Outremer. As I recently said to you, a woman who kills her lord husband is capable of the foulest crimes."

Thomas sat back in shock. "You said there were only rumors, even though you wondered if the tales were true. But there were no charges brought, and thus she is deemed to be innocent. What evidence does Brother Damian have that now convinces you she was guilty of killing her husband? And why did he never tell you this a long time ago?"

"Mistress Hursel was the source. She did not witness the actual deed but saw enough to reasonably conclude what had happened. Later, she told Brother Damian." He looked away, clearly unwilling to answer the second question posed by the monk.

Brother Thomas was not convinced by a witness who *did not see* but *reasonably concluded*. "And you both have cause to say Mistress Hursel was a credible witness? Convince me, Father. I see only a woman who may have wished to tell vile tales of a mistress who had dismissed her from service."

Now the man was squirming. "Yes, she carried tales, Brother! The woman was vicious, loved to ruin or humiliate as many as she could, and..." His expression seemed to beg for understanding. "...asked for coin to remain silent."

Thomas tried to remain calm. The news that Amicia might actually have killed her husband bothered him more than he cared to admit. The butcher's widow was despicable, but she could have come to see Prioress Amicia that day with the intent to threaten her with exposure, or perhaps to suggest how a whispered hint might ruin the prioress' reputation if Mistress Hursel were not given the full charity she demanded for silence.

The other thought that troubled him was a practical one. If Amicia had killed her husband, it was when she was younger and stronger, but the deed would still have required more force than most women had to kill a crusader knight. Maybe Satan had given her strength enough then, and then later on, to kill Mistress Hursel.

Questions about Amicia's innocence began to besiege his mind like an army led by the legendary Salah al-Din. If the butcher's widow threatened to tell her tale about Amicia's husband's death to the Prior of England, might Amicia have feared a penalty that would cause her family loss of honor? Did the woman have children who would suffer? Yet any conviction for murder brought shame. Why fear the earlier one, now that she was vowed to God and under Church authority, when the consequences of killing Mistress Hursel were just as onerous?

Thomas stopped the roaring conflict in his mind by settling on a simple question. "Did she do something to you, Father?"

"It seems she did, Brother, although she never came to me for money, and I never learned exactly what my crime was. Yet I did suffer for it."

Thomas asked him to explain.

"As we all are, I am a wicked man, but my sins are regularly acknowledged, confessed, and I have done penance. So I was surprised one day when my brother came to me and demanded I tell him the great sin his wife had committed, one which I had failed to tell him."

Thomas nodded encouragement when the priest hesitated.

"I said truthfully that I knew of no such thing. But he was drunk, as he often was, and said that Mistress Hursel had told him that his wife had confided her foul sin to me. He demanded to know all the details she had revealed, even if it was in confession. Fool that I was, I did not tell him that she had never confessed to me as her priest. Instead, I reminded him that confessions were for God's ears only. He pulled aside my hair and pointed to my ear. Then he held me down and sliced off a large portion. Since the sin first came to my ear before it ever went to God, he announced, it deserved death for being tainted with wickedness. Had I not screamed, I fear he would have done more than this." He exposed his mutilated ear.

Thomas was horrified. "He was violent when drunk?"

"As brothers, we were as different as chalk and cheese. I chose God as my liege lord. More than most dutiful knights, he reveled in war. He was always prone to violence. Drunk, he could wade through an army of infidels, real or imagined, with his bare fists and leave them screaming for their mothers."

"Did he tell you what this secret was?"

"No. Two of his men heard my cries and rescued me. One of them told me later, as a physician staunched my bleeding, that they often rescued men from his wrath."

"And when he became sober?"

"He mocked me and said that, as a man of God, I should not get into fights. His jest sounds crueler than it was. I was sure he did not recall what had happened. I left within the hour that day for the commandery and returned only once thereafter to see him buried." Pasche tried to smile. "As you see, Brother, I have no reason to want to kill Mistress Hursel, for I never learned what I was supposed to know yet did not. As for revenge over this ear, I could argue that I am a priest and have rejected such sins. That, you might not believe. But it was my brother who injured me, not Mistress Hursel, and I was here when he died."

"Other than Prioress Amicia, is there anyone else here who had cause to kill Mistress Hursel? Did the woman know some secret about Brother Damian or Prioress Emelyne which they did not want anyone to know?"

Pasche shook his head. "Not that I am aware. The only one who had grounds to kill Mistress Hursel was Prioress Amicia if the tale that she had murdered her husband was true."

Thomas mulled this over. There seemed to be no proof that Amicia had killed her husband. Mistress Hursel did not even claim to have witnessed it. Subtle hints can be just as damning, he thought, but I still find no reason to think the former prioress is guilty of both deaths.

Unless, of course, Mistress Hursel had come to tell her that she now had evidence that Amicia had killed her husband. Or, he thought, had she committed this other unknown crime for which this priest had almost lost his ear? Or had Amicia's husband misunderstood something Mistress Hursel told him because he was drunk at the time?

Once again, he opted to ask a question to stop the horde of doubts plaguing him. "Who killed Brother Martin?"

The priest stared at him. "You did lie to Brother Damian. He said you had."

"Would you trust a man who had set two spies on you?"

Blushing, Pasche turned away.

"Brother Martin was the other."

Pasche sat back, his eyes wide. "It was you! You killed the youth for what he was doing!"

"How could I? I was either waiting for Brother Martin to take me to the preceptory or I was with you when he died. Lest you think I might have slipped away to commit the crime before you arrived to accompany me, I believe you will find at least one lay brother was in my company."

"Then I do not know. Surely you are wrong about Brother Martin's death."

"It is difficult to ignore a smashed skull."

Bending his head, Pasche began to weep softly.

"Why did you avoid the corpse, Father? You knew your duty to shrive him."

Now he began to sob. "He was such a sweet boy," he gasped.

Thomas waited.

Taking a deep breath, Pasche rubbed at his eyes. "When he first came to us, he had no vocation, wept piteously, and longed to return to his family. I taught him to catch fish in the ponds for our suppers. He found joy in that and clung to me like a father." Again his cheeks turned pink. "He was an innocent, but I feared the Devil and knew that men often fall into great sin with each other when womanish emotions chase away our manly reason. So I grew stern and turned away from him, hoping he would seek God, not me, for strength." The priest looked sad but forced a smile. "Of late he had fallen more in love with God. I often witnessed him on his knees for hours in prayer."

"Why avoid his dead body?"

"I feared the Devil had again draped his soul in melancholy, and he had committed self-murder." The priest hiccupped a sob.

And you feared it was your fault, Thomas thought. "Brother Martin was murdered. We know the crime was not committed by Sister Amicia, by you, or by me. Was it Brother Damian?"

"Never!" Father Pasche leapt up in horror. "Go back to your own priory and leave us in peace! The death of Mistress Hursel was a blessing from God. You must have misread the injury to Brother Martin's skull." He rubbed a hand over his eyes. "Maybe God is punishing us for our sins, but none of us killed either person." With that, the priest stumbled and pushed his way out of the grass and fled down the path in the direction of the commandery.

Thomas did not follow. Left alone with the soft wind and gentle songs of God's creatures, Thomas knew he now had even less reason to do as the priest had begged.

The relationships of three people here were tangled. Prioress Amicia had been married to Father Pasche's brother, and that brother had been a comrade-in-arms to Brother Damian. If Mistress Hursel had served in the household of Amicia and her husband, and learned secrets no one wanted revealed, it was likely she knew something about Brother Damian as well.

So far, the monk thought with less conviction than he would like, I am beginning to conclude that the commander is the one most likely to have killed both the butcher's widow and the young lay brother. But how could the man have done so?

Thomas rubbed at his eyes in frustration. How would he be able to find evidence that Brother Damian was in the priory when the butcher's widow was killed or was with Brother Martin at the right time?

Chapter Thirty-one

Will I never be freed from this troublesome maid? Prioress Emelyne thought, as Janeta shuffled into her chamber.

Of late, she had noticed that the woman reeked of sweat and her breath was often foul as if she had just vomited. With disgust, she observed that her robes were stained, worn, and badly mended. Even the pouch at her waist was sloppily patched. Had this maid never learned to ply a needle properly? Of course, her former mistress could no longer provide donated or even new clothing, humble in cut and modest in quality though it might be.

Struggling to contain her annoyance and think more charitably, Emelyne decided she could find her a newer robe amongst those they were planning to donate to the poor. It would be a mercy.

Janeta fell to her knees and bowed her head to the ground.

"Stand up! I am neither the Queen of Heaven nor of England and thus unworthy of such reverence."

Janeta crawled to her feet but still kept her eyes lowered.

"You are weeping. What has happened?" Emelyne glanced at the rolls and charters still cluttering her floor and tried not to grow angry even as her stomach clenched in frustration over yet another delay in her work.

"My lady, there is a murderer here. I beg you to find me a position outside this priory."

Emelyne blinked. "I do not understand, my child. The only murderer is your mistress, and she is under guard."

"No, my lady. Brother Martin was killed."

"His death was an accident. There is no reason to fear anyone else will suffer a violent death."

The maid shook her head vigorously. "No, he was killed. I have heard the talk."

Emelyne was not pleased to learn this. Who was spreading that tale? She did not know who had found the lay brother's body nor who was present when Brother Thomas examined the corpse. But the monk had declared it an accident. It was true that her brother believed otherwise, and he had told only Father Pasche in the privacy of his chambers at the commandery. Both men she had always trusted to keep secrets. Why would that change now? She must confirm their silence, but she did not see how this tale of murder could have come from them.

As for the Tyndal monastics, she was certain Prioress Eleanor had not spread such a story, confined as she was to her chambers. Whatever quarrel she might have with the Prioress of Tyndal, she was also convinced she could trust her discretion. And why would Brother Thomas spread the tale since he had concealed the manner of death in the first place? She doubted it was he. The only member of the trio she did not have confidence in was the sub-infirmarian. Had she mentioned the monk's true opinion to her prioress in Janeta's hearing after that highly questionable consultation near the fishponds? She had little trust in the prudence of Sister Anne.

"Who is telling this?" Emelyne asked.

"I cannot say. I overheard women talking but did not see their faces."

Or else you do not want to tell me, the prioress thought, noting the maid's sudden change of color, and felt a flash of anger.

"I fear for my life! You must save me!"

"There is no reason to believe you are in danger here."

"Mistress Hursel was murdered, now Brother Martin. The nuns convicted my mistress of the first crime, but someone else has shed blood here. This priory is not safe." She reached out her hands to beg. "Find me a place far away from Mynchen Buckland!"

"We thought you might want to remain here, child, once your mistress died. I would accept you as a lay sister."

"I cannot remain where I am in danger. Please!" Janeta began to cry.

"There is no place for you in the world," Emelyne said, more harshly than she intended.

Janeta's eyes grew wide with horror as she sobbed even louder.

The prioress put a hand on her shoulder. "I know of no one who wishes a servant," she said.

"Even marriage," Janeta whimpered. "A husband would protect me."

Emelyne looked at the maid with amazement. This last remark proved just how irrational the woman was. Arranging a secular marriage was not something prioresses did.

"Calm yourself," she said. "Go to the chapel and pray for God's peace. Seek advice from Father Pasche. You will soon realize that staying here is a far better thing than going into the world. If you fear wickedness, there is far more there. You are safest here, both body and soul."

The terror and grief in the maid's eyes were undiminished. "Forgive me, my lady, but you are wrong." Then she leapt to her feet and escaped from the chamber.

Emelyne sat back and stared at the door that Janeta had carelessly left open in her flight.

A nun stepped inside and grasped the handle but hesitated before shutting it. "Do you have any instructions for me?"

"Only that I wish to be left in peace until the next Office."

The prioress reached for another accounting roll.

Chapter Thirty-two

Eleanor stood near the window, took a deep breath of the spring air, and felt her spirits revive. She might be weary of this game and long to return to her priory, but she was ever more determined to discover the truth in this knotted puzzle. Even though she tried to convince herself that she would be satisfied just to find enough evidence to cleanse the dying woman from her undeserved conviction, she wanted the murderer found and punished as well.

Yet the frustration of thinking in circles remained. All she needed was one small detail to set her on a new path. Just one.

After a knock on the door to announce her presence, Sister Anne entered and immediately asked, "Have you thought more about what we might have failed to see?"

"I fear we know so very little," the prioress replied, but her voice suggested less discouragement than thought.

"We are therefore no closer to finding out who did the killings." With little interest, Anne looked down at the activity in the courtyard below. Then she grasped the meaning of her prioress' tone. "Or are we?"

"The death of Brother Martin may have made those who were willing to accept Prioress Amicia's conviction on weak evidence less eager to do so."

Eleanor watched a large bird of indeterminate color land on the nearby roof and aimlessly hop about. The creature reminded her of what she felt she was doing with the facts of this murder, and that almost made her smile.

She turned to Sister Anne. "If we assume that is the case, we might be able to prove Prioress Amicia innocent, even if we don't find the killer."

"Once again, I cannot believe you are willing to let a murderer go free."

"I am not and pray daily that God will bring me the needed insights." Eleanor glanced at the small altar near the bed.

"Our primary suspects are the former prioress, the current one, Brother Damian, and Father Pasche. You mentioned the steward. Do you think he is likely?"

"Brother Thomas found him innocuous, dutiful, and cheerful. Had he seen anything in his brief contact that suggested a darker aspect, he would have told you. As for the others, there are so many reasons why they could not have killed both. We have spoken of all that."

Anne nodded.

"Both Prioress Emelyne and her brother seem prone to anger. Brother Thomas has seen the commander be sharp in speech. But we do not know if either had any cause to kill. Brother Damian showed great sorrow over the death of Brother Martin and even asked Brother Thomas to examine the body. That suggests the commander was more concerned about the death than anything our monk might have been doing and, on reflection, makes me waver in my suspicion that he is the murderer."

"Then let us set him aside for the moment. What about the priest or the prioress?"

Eleanor started to pace but stopped, obviously annoyed with such restricted and boringly repetitive activity. "Prioress Emelyne seemed willing enough to let Prioress Amicia take the blame for the crime. I assume her brother did as well, since we have not heard otherwise. But they also wanted her to be granted mercy. Instead of letting the Prior cast her from the preceptory to die a hard and lonely death, they begged him to grant her the mercy of remaining here with a priest, medical care, and in an austere but comfortable cell. What does that suggest?"

"We might assume it was an act of mercy because she is dying."

"Or that her conviction brought some desired result," Eleanor said, "yet they wished her no ill. I have not met Prioress Emelyne's brother, but I do not think she is a monster, bred from Satan's loins. It is quite possible that they both know she is innocent and even feel some guilt for allowing her to take the blame."

"You have told me that Prioress Emelyne would have been chosen to replace Prioress Amicia on her death anyway. Might there be a reason why an earlier appointment was desired?"

"A well raised question."

"Brother Thomas did mention that the former prioress had chosen to send more priory income to Clerkenwell rather than · do needed maintenance here. Brother Martin had thought the election of Prioress Emelyne would change that."

"Yet I fail to see how improving the fishponds would warrant the extreme measure of letting an innocent woman be convicted of murder. There must be another purpose, but I fail to see it, unless they know who did the crime and wish to protect that person."

"And that would make them culpable." Anne thought for a moment. "Father Pasche? He has long been the priest here and may have gained their loyalty."

"About him I have made no firm conclusions." Eleanor sat on the bed, her legs dangling like a child's, and sighed. "I miss my cot at Tyndal," she said. "I am too small for horses, fine furniture, and large beds."

"And you miss your cat," Sister Anne said. "When Arthur sits on your lap, he often proves inspirational."

Eleanor laughed. "At the moment, the sight of one of Tyndal's accounting rolls might supply good motivation to think beyond what we have been doing."

"What can we do?"

"As I said, we cannot stay here much longer. I must stop pretending to have no interest in this matter and humble myself."

"Is that wise? Might it even be dangerous?"

"It is wise if I choose the right person to approach. It will be perilous if I am wrong in my judgment." She held up her hand before her friend had the chance to respond. "If I fear I am talking to the murderer, I shall say nothing about my suspicions and confess only that Prioress Amicia has begged my help to prove her innocence, not find the murderer. I shall have to think quickly, but I will do nothing to imperil our own safety and impede our departure as soon as possible."

"What do you want me to do?"

Eleanor started to reply and then gestured toward the door. "Where is Janeta?"

"She told me that she had a favor to beg from the prioress."

"Perhaps she is finished. If so, you must summon Prioress Emelyne. Tell her that I am much improved but must confer with her."

Anne hesitated as if wanting to argue but chose to say nothing and walked to the door.

Eleanor slid off the bed. "We have not always had much time to talk alone. Before you go, can you think of anything you may have discovered or found curious? I would welcome the most petty or even an arcane detail."

Anne turned around, her expression thoughtful. "I think I have mentioned everything I thought pertinent, but there was one thing from this last visit with Brother Thomas. It probably means nothing, but I think Janeta is with child. She is ill in the mornings. I believe she vomits because I can smell it on her breath after. She claims this occurs before her courses, yet I have not noticed that metallic smell women often have while bleeding. Her profuse sweating is not uncommon in pregnant women either. Without examining her, I could be wrong, but, if she is, that would explain her troubled manner. Bearing a bastard child would not make her life very easy with a mistress who is dying and no hope of any employment where a child would be welcomed."

"This news might also imperil the likelihood of her acceptance as a lay sister. How very much alone she must feel," Eleanor replied. "This news saddens me deeply."

Then she walked to the window, looked down on the courtyard, and fell into a profound silence.

Chapter Thirty-three

It was Eleanor who opened the door when Prioress Emelyne knocked.

"Let us speak alone," she said to Sister Anne, and then stood aside as the Hospitaller prioress brushed past her with bristling antagonism.

When the door was shut, Emelyne spun around. "God has kindly healed you more swiftly than any mortal might suppose." She stared at her nemesis' foot.

"Would you like some wine?" Eleanor smiled hospitably.

"As I thought you understood, I have little time for idle conversation," the prioress snapped.

"Nor is that why I asked you to come."

"When do you plan to leave? It would be a courtesy to let us know so we might make the proper arrangements for the remainder of your time here, as well as for your departure." Each word could not have been cut off more sharply if it had been sliced with a knife.

"Shall we stop circling each other like warring cats, Prioress Emelyne?"

The woman blinked, but her glare did not waver.

Eleanor handed her a full mazer. "We are both vowed to God's service and must therefore cast aside many earthly desires and bonds. Is it not our duty to strive toward a better union with His ultimate perfection?"

Now looking perplexed, Emelyne took the wine. "I did not come for a sermon," she muttered.

Eleanor ignored her. "Yet we are flawed creatures and often fall victim to our own frailties." Then she stopped before continuing in a conciliatory tone. "I did not ask you to leave your work to hear me preach. As a woman guilty of profound faults, my purpose was to beg your help in a matter we both are vowed to uphold: justice pleasing to God, not to mortals."

Emelyne opened her mouth to retort. A high color flowed over her cheeks, and she said nothing, stared into her mazer, and then drained it.

Eleanor did not let this silence linger. "You know that Sister Amicia is innocent of murder. I did not have to tell you that. Your conscience has always known it."

Turning her back, the prioress walked to the ewer, put down her mazer, and bowed her head. "You lied to me," she said.

Eleanor noticed that the woman's voice trembled but not, she thought, with anger. "Or did God send me at this particular time and provide a way to keep me here so we could join hands and together find the strength—something no one person could do alone—to execute His will in this matter? His ways are mysterious, as we all know."

Now Emelyne's hands were shaking, and she could not fill her mazer.

Eleanor took the cup, poured the wine, and gently offered it to her.

Ignoring the gesture, Emelyne covered her face.

"I am not casting stones, least of all at you," Eleanor murmured, setting the cup aside, "for I am not without sin."

Collapsing to her knees, the prioress began to weep inconsolably.

Eleanor knelt beside her and took her into her arms like a mother would a wounded child.

Finally conquering her tears, Emelyne sat back and wiped her cheeks dry. "I know your reputation well. God surely guides you, and I have no cause to doubt your conclusion. How did you determine her innocence?"

"When a murder occurs in a cloister garth, it is a frightening thing for nuns. Gossip may be one of woman's many faults, but it seems to calm our fears to share news. I learned that lesson soon after I arrived at Tyndal Priory when the same tragedy as you have suffered occurred there."

"I had not heard that tale," Emelyne said with surprise.

"It was then I also discovered the value of listening to every word spoken, even the lowest whisper, and balancing the merits of what I had learned in order to better rule our priory. It is a truth you surely know as well, but you are laden with the hard burdens of taking over from the former prioress under difficult circumstances. You have not had the opportunity to ponder tales, as I have as I lay idle in my bed."

"Sister Anne overheard these tales as she walked in the garth?" Emelyne spoke with sad resignation.

Despite her delight over this conclusion, Eleanor only nodded in response before adding, "And you told me that your former prioress was mortally ill. I confess I wondered how a dying woman could kill one presumably so much stronger than she."

"But why did she allow us to condemn her? Why did she not defend herself?" Emelyne's questions were asked in a tone of curiosity rather than malice. The tears conquered, she also seemed to have banished her initial outrage with her guest.

Eleanor stood and offered her hand to help her fellow prioress rise. "Nor did she confess. Does that not suggest she wanted to avoid an outright lie? Had she been guilty, she would have admitted to the sin."

"Had she been innocent, she would have sworn to that."

"Unless she had a reason other than the murder for not defending herself. Was she not reputed to be devout?"

Emelyne agreed.

"Perhaps she was so horrified by finding a woman killed on God's hallowed earth that she took the desecration on herself. As the prioress, she might have believed the crime occurred because she herself had somehow deeply offended God."

"I had not thought of that." Emelyne accepted her refilled mazer, walked to the window, and sipped.

"Sister Amicia is dying. I am sure that, on her deathbed, she would not lie to the priest. If she believed she was to blame for the befouling of this priory because of her own transgressions, she would confess those as well. I find her physical frailty a stronger argument for innocence than her refusal to deny guilt a reason to conclude she had killed Mistress Hursel."

The leader of Mynchen Buckland priory looked over her shoulder, her eyes dulled with sadness. "I, too, have sinned."

"As have we all," Eleanor replied, "but your confession must be given to your priest, as my wickedness shall be to mine."

Walking back to the ewer, Emelyne poured wine into a fresh cup and offered it with a bow of humility to the Prioress of Tyndal. "In the spirit of our mutual desire for truth, I offer you this admission, one you must hear before I take it to my priest."

Eleanor took the cup as the gesture of appeasement it was meant to be.

"It was Father Pasche who insisted that our former prioress be accused of murder and tried in Chapter. Before the evidence was heard, my brother also came to me and argued for her guilt. He said that her refusal to deny her crime was as good as a confession but conceded that, if she did declare her innocence and gave convincing testimony on her own behalf, he would agree that she was most likely innocent."

"That argument has merit." Eleanor hid her dissatisfaction with Brother Damian's approach. Of course, she should find out precisely why Amicia had refused to defend herself, but she was fully convinced it held no suggestion of guilt in the murder of the butcher's widow. It seemed more important to find out why both the priest and Brother Damian had been so insistent on finding her guilty.

Emelyne misread what she saw in her fellow prioress' face, and her lips twitched with a brief smile. "As we each know, elder brothers have the power of persuasion." She sighed and put down her mazer. "And thus I sat in Chapter with my other sisters in God and listened to Sister Richolda say that our prioress was too frail to have committed the crime, while Father Pasche argued that Satan can give any mortal great strength to sin if the soul is weak." She bowed her head. "And I have since learned that the Prince of Darkness can also blind the soul to truth with the brilliant fire of ambition. Thus I failed to raise any questions that might have led to her acquittal, or at least to find there was no good evidence to convict her without further inquiry."

Her expression devoid of any censure, Eleanor waited for her to continue.

"My brother and I both knew that my election to head this priory was almost certain. Many of us had been aware of Prioress Amicia's failing health for some time. Discussion amongst the nuns about who should be our next prioress had already begun. My name was the most frequently mentioned."

"Such talk reasonably occurs when an election seems imminent."

"My brother was eager that I be chosen to lead Mynchen Buckland as soon as possible. My own desire to rise to the position was equally strong. Neither of us saw any cause for the election not to occur sooner, in view of Prioress Amicia's poor health. If she lingered, but was incapable of functioning in her position, someone would have to ease her burdens until she died. It was better, we both agreed, if I could be elected before that happened and provide stability in leadership."

"And thus you agreed on her guilt."

"It was not that simple. Neither of us admitted the strength of our mutual ambition. Instead, we spoke of it as a wise course of action. There would be no harm done. Prioress Amicia has no children in the world and no close kin. We thought it likely she was guilty. Who else could it have been?"

"Murder is a vile crime. It so defiles the soul that even God must find it hard to forgive."

"But my brother and I also agreed that we would beg the Prior of England for mercy in view of her illness." She looked at

Eleanor with pleading eyes. "If she were innocent, God would know that as well!"

"Did Brother Damian say why he especially wanted you to be elected prioress here so soon? You and I both know there was another motive beyond the practical."

"Family honor," she said. "To have a brother knight named a commander of men while his sister is elected the commander of women would bring credit to our kin."

Eleanor was not convinced but said nothing. To head this tiny commandery of men was not a great honor for Brother Damian, although having his sister lead the only preceptory of Hospitaller nuns in England might be. Ambition is an odd sin. Often the prize glows brightly only in the eyes of the sinner.

Emelyne bridled at her companion's silence. "Lest you wish to accuse me, I did not kill Mistress Hursel. When the crime was committed, I was in the chapel with several other nuns, praying for the souls of our dead benefactors. Ask for confirmation, if you will, but I beg that it be done privately."

Biting back a sigh of relief that there were witnesses to the innocence of Prioress Emelyne, a woman she could not like but did see grounds to respect, Eleanor assured her that such corroboration would not be needed.

But now she prayed that Emelyne might have an insight that would allow her to see how the murder of the butcher's widow was linked to that of the young lay brother. "Mistress Hursel was not the only one killed. Brother Martin was, as well," Eleanor said, hoping this revelation would so shock the prioress that she would say something important without realizing what it meant.

"That was an accident! Brother Thomas confirmed it."

Eleanor caught Emelyne's inability to look at her when she spoke those words. "Brother Thomas now believes otherwise," she replied tactfully. "Perhaps he spoke too quickly after he saw your brother's immense grief over the boy's death. An accidental death is hard enough to bear, but, if the young man had committed self-murder, might that have caused your brother even greater sorrow? I fear the good monk may have chosen compassion for your brother over his better judgment."

"I should have been informed of his change of opinion. I was not, nor, I believe, was my brother."

The complaint was valid, but Eleanor noted there was little bite of reproach in Emelyne's words.

"And I am doing so now. I have not known of this long. Sister Anne and I have had few opportunities to discuss everything she and Brother Thomas spoke about that evening. As you know, Sister Anne joins all your nuns for prayer. The hours pass quickly in performing our duties to God."

"Are you saying you think the two deaths are linked?"

"Most likely."

Prioress Emelyne rubbed at the corners of her reddened eyes. "Then I shall directly reply to your concerns about any guilt I might own in this second death. I am overwhelmed with the work of taking over priory business. On occasion, I have missed the hours of prayer and even taken my meals in my chambers. Under no circumstances could I have gone to the fishponds and pushed Brother Martin into the water. Ask the nun who stays outside my chamber door until the last Office of the day."

A good response, Eleanor thought, nor does she know about the crushed skull. "Can you think of anyone who might have done so?"

"Not my brother. He loved Brother Martin like a son. Your monk saw him weeping over his body. And ask yourself how easy it would be for Damian, with only one hand, to drown him? As for Father Pasche, he was either with my brother in chambers or in the company of your monk, unless I am mistaken about the time the lay brother drowned. The lad was an innocent. I cannot imagine why anyone would have killed him."

Recalling what Brother Thomas had said, Eleanor wondered if the youth was not quite as innocent as he was assumed to be. She chose not to say this and instead asked, "Do you know of any reason why someone would have wanted to kill Mistress Hursel?"

"I have heard that she was not well-loved in the village, but I cared little for the telling of idle tales and had no interest in learning why. Since she never came to our priory, I did not meet her." With a frown, she looked down at her mazer, realized there was still wine in it, and drank. "My brother knew more of her ways and had no fondness for her, once calling her a collector of secrets. He was friends with the husband of our former prioress. Damian was very loyal to him, for it was he who saved my brother's life after his hand was cut off. When he learned Mistress Hursel had been dismissed from service, he was pleased and I wondered if he thought the woman was telling scurrilous lies about his friend. When Damian heard the woman had married our local butcher, he was angry for days."

Eleanor dared not ask but tilted her head with a questioning look and prayed the prioress would not be offended.

Emelyne read the question well. "Nay, my brother could not have killed the woman. He and I share a tendency to choler, but his rages destroy only doors and candlesticks. His words do sometimes wound people, but that is not murder."

Eleanor knew it was not the time to debate that conclusion. Emelyne chose to continue the defense of her brother. "In truth, I thought he should have joined a more contemplative Order. As a boy, he was devout but never showed a warrior's enthusiasm for battle. Perhaps he would have become a Benedictine, had one of our uncles not risen to high rank in this Order, and I suspect our father may have made the choice for Damian."

"Perhaps he longed to regain Jerusalem and enter the gates as a pilgrim."

"Nay!" she snapped. "It was because our father would have mocked him as a womanly boy if he did not take up arms as a knight." Emelyne suddenly drew back, realizing she had said more than she wished. "But that is irrelevant to the crimes here."

To keep peace, Eleanor simply nodded. "And Father Pasche? Did he know Mistress Hursel?"

"Perhaps you have already learned this, but our priest is the brother of Prioress Amicia's dead husband." She waited for a reaction but saw none. "Yet he has resided here for many years and entered the priesthood before his brother married her. On rare occasions, he visited them. I doubt he even knew who Mistress Hursel was among the many servants there."

"One last question, Prioress Emelyne. Sister Anne found a red-jeweled ring with a gold band that was lost in the cloister garth and showed it to Sister Richolda in hopes she might know the owner. The infirmarian recognized it as belonging to your former prioress and returned it to her. Did you ever see it or know anything of its origins?"

Emelyne looked up as she thought about the question. "I once saw her take it out of her pouch and kiss it but did not know why she kept it after taking vows. In our Order, we are allowed to keep a small item or two that reminds us of a loved one, usually now dead. Perhaps it had belonged to her mother or had been a gift from her husband? But just before Amicia's conviction, I noticed Janeta with it. She was gazing at the ring in the light of a window, and then she put it into her own pouch. At the time, I wondered if she had stolen the ring, but I had never heard any rumors that she was a thief. So I concluded that our prioress lost it, the maid found it, and was planning to return it. I thought no further on it."

With that, Prioress Eleanor thanked Prioress Emelyne for the help she had given. Then she said that she and her monastics would be leaving the next day. "I beg that you find a way to release Amicia without delay and let her die without the infamy of a cruel verdict," she added.

"You are leaving without finding the murderer?" Emelyne was as surprised as Sister Anne had been.

And that might have amused Prioress Eleanor if she had not been so grieved over the next step she must take. "If it so pleases Him, God may yet reveal the killer, but I will not abuse your charity beyond tomorrow," she replied. "Should He enlighten me with the identity of the murderer, I swear you will not be kept in ignorance long, even if circumstances demand I take swift action before doing so."

Emelyne frowned as if insulted, then seemed to change her mind and nodded acquiescence. "I shall do as you ask about our former prioress. It would also relieve me if she were able to die with the knowledge that we have all found her innocent."

"I must ask a favor of Janeta," Eleanor said. "Can you spare her for a short while?"

Emelyne agreed, eager to return to the interrupted review of her accounting rolls. "I shall be in my chambers, should you need me, as may my brother. I have found something troubling that requires consultation with him."

Eleanor firmly shut the door behind the woman so she might have some brief moments of prayer. To reach the end of this sad journey, she needed all the strength God could give her. She may have begun with a kind oath that she would do her best to prove Prioress Amicia innocent, but what she must do now filled her with bitter sorrow.

Chapter Thirty-four

The maid's skin was sallow, and the circles underlining her eyes were like bruises. Staring at the floor, she resembled a child waiting to be whipped.

With interest, Eleanor noted that she had folded her hands under her belly, although there was no evident sign that Janeta was with child.

"The ring which your mistress gave you and you lost has been found."

Janeta did not look up nor did she speak.

"Sister Anne found it in the cloister garth, under a thorny shrub and behind the bench where Mistress Hursel was killed." Eleanor reached out and touched the mended pouch at the maid's waist. "Did the bush tear this in your hurry to escape?"

The maid raised one hand, pressed it against her belly, and whimpered.

In that moment, Eleanor was filled with agonizing grief over what she was doing and begged God to give her a sign that she was horribly wrong. Yet she knew she had little choice but to continue. "Who got you with child?"

Janeta cried out and turned as if she wanted to flee.

Eleanor grabbed her shoulder and, despite the difference in their sizes and strength, easily spun her around.

With a howl of pain, the maid fell to her knees and began to pound the floor with her fists.

Kneeling beside her, the prioress spoke gently. "Was it Father Pasche? Brother Damian?" She took a deep breath and grasped the young woman more firmly. "Or was it Brother Martin?" Lifting her head, Janeta stared at her tormentor. Her eyes glittered as if reflecting the eternity of flames she faced. "We did not mean to sin," she murmured. "We often spoke when I went to the commandery with messages for Brother Damian. One day I took the path from the road to the fishponds and saw him surveying the damage done by the spring rains and rising water. He told me he feared the fish could not survive in the foul weeds and mud, and his cheeks were damp with tears." Gasping, she bent over and wrapped her arms around herself. "He was so caring and gentle."

The sins committed in this tragedy were dire, but Eleanor found herself begging God for a kinder resolution.

"I longed to comfort him, took him into my arms, and gave him a kiss on his cheek. He kissed me back. I gave him gentle caresses to soothe his sorrow, and he began to touch me as well." For a fleeting moment, Janeta's face softened with happiness. "I chased away his sadness, He eased my loneliness. But the Devil saw us and laughed at our foolish innocence. He filled our bodies with his hellish fire until our longing to grow closer became more than we could bear." Grief again overcame her. "As we coupled, we felt no sin. Instead, we thought we had found the Garden of Eden and soon fell asleep in each other's arms."

Eleanor wanted to tell the maid how much she understood, even if the joy she had felt herself had only been in sinful dreams. But instead she sat back and withdrew her hand from the woman's shoulder. "Did you meet often to lie together?" she asked and regretted her harsh tone.

Janeta flinched, and her lips twisted with hostility. "We never did again. When we awoke, Mistress Hursel was standing over us, laughing at our nakedness. She swore we would pay for our wickedness but promised to wait until she had a price she wanted us to pay. Then she left. It was only then that he and I looked at each other and felt the shame of Adam and Eve after they had tasted the forbidden apple."

"So you quickened with Brother Martin's child," Eleanor whispered.

The maid nodded and caressed her belly with protective tenderness.

"Why did you not confide in your mistress that Brother Martin had broken his vows with you and what Mistress Hursel threatened? Or had Prioress Amicia been convicted by then?"

"How could I? She was dying. When she told me, she gave me the ring so I might sell it. It was the only thing she could bequeath, but then she begged me to enter the priory as a lay sister. She had no use for the world and urged me to abandon it after her death. I had not yet realized I was with child. When I did, I could not burden her with all my sins."

"And then Mistress Hursel came to the priory?"

"Just after she arrived and asked for my mistress, she told me my time had come to pay her price. She was certain I had been paid well to keep Prioress Amicia's secrets. I told her I had never been paid to remain silent about anything. She accused me of lying, said she knew better, and swore she would tell my mistress how I had committed sacrilege by seducing a man vowed to God. If I did not immediately bring her the coin I had hidden away, she would make sure I was dismissed that very day for whoring in God's priory."

Eleanor sat without moving and wanted to weep. The time for tears, however, would come later.

"I knelt and swore I would find a way to pay her if she did not tell my mistress. It must be now, she said, for she had no reason to trust me after I had just lied to her. So I agreed and started to leave when Satan once more took possession of me. I turned around and told Mistress Hursel that her chain was coming undone and I would fix it. I slipped behind her, stabbed her with my dining knife, tossed that aside, and fled."

"But you went to your mistress to announce the arrival of the woman you had just killed."

Janeta nodded, her expression dulled by remembering events she did not fully understand herself. "Father Pasche had just arrived, and she told me to provide refreshment until she returned. He insisted I take him to the garth because he also knew of Mistress Hursel. I did, and we found my mistress with the corpse and blood on her hands."

Janeta's tone is so cold, Eleanor thought, as if the maid has lost all feeling. "You let your mistress take the blame for the crime. Had she not been good to you? Why did you allow this?"

Janeta's eyes were now bereft of sense or emotion. "Satan closed my mouth when she refused to defend herself, my lady. He must have done so, for she always treated me with kindness while I served her."

Eleanor went on. "Did the Devil also lead you to kill Brother Martin, a man who may have sinned with you but never deserved that fate?"

The icy hardness of the maid's expression shattered into grief-stricken horror.

Chapter Thirty-five

Prioress Emelyne did not rise when her brother entered her chambers, nor did she speak. Instead, she opened two documents, resting one finger at a particular spot on each, and stared at him in rage.

"Why did you call me here, Sister? I have a corpse to bury."

"Is this why you committed murder?" She poked at the parchments.

"You jabber like most women. I have neither the time nor the patience to humor you."

"I am not prattling, Brother, but you are a liar and a thief. I only pray you have not committed even greater sins."

He paled as he realized the documents she held down were accounting rolls.

"Explain, if you can, why the Prior of England sent a message to Prioress Amicia wondering at the sudden drop in revenue from the income for which you were responsible." She banged her fist on one roll. "Yet the income sent from this preceptory was suddenly raised after the receipt of that query to match the lack."

He started to speak.

She waved her hand for silence and bent close to study another document in front of her. "Do not bother repeating what Prioress Amicia sent in justification. I have a copy here. An accounting problem?" She snorted. "The nuns actually owed more and the brothers less?"

His tongue refused to help his lips form words.

"I am sick of lies," she snapped. "Despite the explanation that the drop in your revenue contribution was due to an *accounting problem* between what the nuns owed and your religious, it seems that this interesting imbalance dramatically changed here." She hit the second roll with her other fist. "And lest you wish to argue that I am a foolish woman, incapable of reason, I do recall that this latter change occurred at the time Mistress Hursel married the butcher." She waited a moment. "I verified that fact with a reliable source."

He began to study the rushes on the floor.

"And as you often mention with profound contempt, women chatter like the frivolous creatures we are. So I have learned when Mistress Hursel was banished from Prioress Amicia's service as well as confirming when she married the butcher. These documents suggest that the sudden drop in contributions from the property under your stewardship and the subsequent increase…" With mock amazement, she looked back and forth at the two parchments. "…match the dates of those first and last significant events."

"There is no connection…"

Leaping to her feet, the prioress picked up her cup of wine and threw it at him.

It struck his left shoulder and stained his white cross with a dark hue.

"I have just spoken with Prioress Eleanor. She knows Prioress Amicia is innocent of the crime for which she was convicted. Although you and I both agreed that the evidence against her was weak, you insisted that I vote for her condemnation. Why, Brother? What sin did she discover that made you so eager for her to be found guilty of such a vile wickedness?"

His face was turning red.

She walked up to him until they stood only inches apart. Raising her hand, she slapped him as hard as she could.

He fell back, his hand to his face. "Only our mother did that to me!"

"And she should have done it more often. When our father raged at you for being womanish, she defended you. Yet she never tolerated your lies. I always have, however, being your dutiful and younger sister. No longer, Brother!" She marched back to the table. "What transgressions have you committed?"

As if the blow had drained his strength, Damian staggered to the chair and collapsed into it.

"Tell me the truth now. I am willing to confess my sins in this matter. It is time you did as well."

Trying to regain his control, he waved his hand at her, then looked up with the expression of a child begging mercy from an angry parent. "Wine?" he whimpered.

Shaking her head, she brought him a brimming cup.

Damian gulped at it. "When the Prior sent the message, Prioress Amicia realized something was amiss. Without consulting me, as she ought to have done, she spoke first to the steward who confirmed that the income from commandery lands had not dropped, which meant that only the amount I reported had done so."

"Ought to have done? I think she was wise not to have asked you for your version first. Had I been prioress then, I would have done as you hoped and forced myself to believe whatever lie you chose to tell." She stood with arms folded, but her anger was slowly replaced with deep sorrow.

He drank his wine. "She called me to account." He drank again.

"And knew you were stealing money from the Order. That is clear enough, Brother. Do not try to cover your deed with your usual bluster. I will no longer tolerate it, and the Prior of England will most certainly not."

He looked at her with terror. "You will inform him? My sister would do such a thing to me?"

"What did Prioress Amicia say?"

"You…"

"Answer my question."

"She asked me what I was using the money for. I told her. She found my explanation adequate and promised to protect me." He glared at his sister. "That should suffice."

Emelyne reached over and swatted the cup he held. Wine splashed his face and he cried out from the sting of it in his eyes. "Why were you stealing? Why did she find your reason *sufficient*?"

"May the Prince of Darkness cut into your soul with his claws until you scream for eternity!"

"God will joyfully throw you into his clutches, if you continue to lie about your sins, for He sees transgressions that men do not. With even greater pleasure, the Devil will dig his claws into a part of your body that is far more tender than your soul."

He looked into his cup and drank the remaining wine. "I was paying someone to keep secret something that happened to me in Outremer."

"Mistress Hursel?"

With a growl, he nodded.

"Did you tell Prioress Amicia what the secret was?"

"She insisted. And she swore she would protect me."

"I am baffled." Emelyne glanced at the second roll on the table and then back at her sullen brother. "So Mistress Hursel threatened you with exposure of your foul deed before she came here, yet the payments stopped when she married the butcher?"

Damian snorted. "An honorable thief! She said she had funds enough with her marriage."

"Yet when he died, the butcher left her only a widow's portion, and her stepsons refused to add to her support. Did she come here to exact more money from you? And did you kill her in desperation? And did you want Prioress Amicia to take the blame so she would be discredited and thus unable to expose your secret?"

"I swear by every saint and all the holy names of God that I did not kill anyone, nor did I plan to have your former prioress silenced!" He slid from the chair to his knees and lifted his arms like a pleading beggar. "I confess that it did not grieve me that

Mistress Hursel was dead or that Prioress Amicia might have killed her…"

"You still claim that you thought she had?"

"I had no cause to deliberately cast blame on her. When I told her about the demand for money from the butcher's wife, your prioress understood, saying that Mistress Hursel had tried to do the same with others. At first, I wondered if that was why she had dismissed the woman from her service. Later, I asked myself if she had also been threatened with exposure of a dangerous secret if she did not pay the woman for her silence."

Emelyne did not say anything, and the silence grew unbearable between them. Finally, she asked, "Why should I believe you?" She kept her voice hard but turned her face away so he could not see her traitorous tears. "If Prioress Amicia knew you had a secret worth extortion, you had grounds to kill her as well as the butcher's widow. Letting our prioress be condemned for murder must have suited you well."

"I again swear my innocence! Of course, I felt no grief that she was found guilty, but ask yourself if she did not point to her own guilt by refusing to defend herself. I know of no reason for her to have done that."

"Perhaps she had a reason besides murder for doing so. She was too frail to kill the woman. You knew it as well as I."

"Ask me to do anything, Sister, and I swear to obey."

When she looked back at him, she saw he, too, was weeping, and she softened. "Sweet Brother, we have both committed grave sins. You out of fear of exposure. I out of worldly ambition. We must both atone by admitting our crimes to the Prior of England and accepting whatever punishment he deems proper." She knelt by his side and took his one hand in hers. "Together, we must humble ourselves. God will forgive the penitent, and it is our souls that must be cleansed. What difference does worldly rank matter if we suffer an eternity in Hell?"

"I gave my word to you. I will keep it."

But she heard him grinding his teeth in fury as he said it, and her sympathy vanished. Knowing him well, she was aware that he would find a way out of his oath, leaving her to suffer a hard penance alone. Dropping his hand, she began to pinch his cheeks until he cried out. "Indeed you shall, Brother, for now you must tell me what you did in Outremer that was so terrible that you actually stole money from God to hide it."

"Why should I?" he shouted.

"If you do not, I shall do everything in my power to discover your secret and expose every detail to all and sundry. Might this not be worse than a confession that you paid Mistress Hursel money stolen from God to stay silent about a vague and ancient sin?" She tilted her head. "After all, any such transgression would be one which you must have confessed and served penance for long ago."

And when he told her what he had done, she found she could no longer weep, for all her tears had been shed over things far more deserving.

Chapter Thirty-six

Prioress Eleanor looked at the young woman who lay sprawled on the floor. Rarely had she felt so torn and in need of guidance. Her heart longed to show compassion while her mind argued for unwavering righteousness. Which was closer to God's justice?

But her aunt was dead, and it was impossible to elicit thoughtful advice in an instant from Sister Anne and Brother Thomas. Of all the times she needed time to pray, this was one, but she could not escape to do so. In the silence of her soul, she uttered one short plea to God to grant her wisdom.

Janeta pushed herself from the floor and stood. Her appearance had gone from utter defeat to a sad defiance. "Tell me, my lady, what God would have advised."

"He would not have told you to kill either Mistress Hursel or Brother Martin."

Yet God was not always gentle, she reminded herself. He was the God of mercy but also of battles. Once He had stayed the sun until the Israelites could destroy their enemies. In recent times, the pope had declared it His will that Christian knights reclaim Jerusalem, shedding blood wantonly as needed. Which face of God ruled here?

"Most certainly not Brother Martin," Eleanor added firmly. In that one statement she felt confidence.

Janeta's eyes narrowed, and her lips curled into a sneer. She bit down on a finger until it bled.

In that moment, Eleanor realized that the maid's humors were not just unbalanced. Her fears, sins, and deep grief had turned her wits. Yet the prioress was not worried about her own safety. She was most anxious that she lacked the ability to save the woman's soul.

"When I told him I was with child, he said we must immediately confess our sins and repent. I replied that the penance would be tolerable for him. He might remain in the Order and be given food and shelter. I, on the other hand, must bear a child in the agony of all women cursed by the sins of Eve and then be cast out with the babe to die, beg, or whore." Janeta's words were so bitter that the very air in which they were uttered turned as sharp as a honed blade against the ear.

"Or give up the child," Eleanor said softly. "You might still have remained here."

The maid glanced at her belly and protectively covered it with both hands.

"The Hospitallers would have raised the babe until the age of reason was reached and a decision could be made to serve the Order or go into the world with a skill. They did this in Acre and even earlier in Jerusalem."

As if the two women were speaking different languages, Janeta looked at the prioress in frustration, then shook her head and tried again to explain. "I begged him to wait before confessing, for I wanted to find a path I could take. He readily agreed and said he would pray for a while longer, asking God to forgive us both for our wickedness. He urged me to do the same and said He might give one of us a sign and guide us in the right direction if our prayers were sincere enough."

A wise choice, Eleanor thought. Although the pair had sinned, their errors were pardonable. As for the child Janeta must bear, it would be agony for her to surrender it, but even then there might have been a way to…

Janeta's eyes faded into blankness. "Then Mistress Hursel came here, and I killed her."

Eleanor felt a flash of anger, not at Janeta but with Mistress Hursel. It was the butcher's widow who had, with evil joy, led Satan by the hand into this priory. The maid and Brother Martin may have lain together, but their transgression was common enough. Many a babe had appeared months after what had begun with a few innocuous caresses.

Whatever compassion the Order might have shown two innocents had been destroyed by the butcher's wife. Janeta had now committed two horrendous crimes because of this older woman's cruelty. In her heart, Eleanor felt Mistress Hursel had deserved her fate, but it was Janeta who would suffer for implementing it.

"When I took a message to Brother Damian from Prioress Emelyne, I saw Brother Martin outside his door. He told me when to meet him at the ponds. His face glowed with joy. I felt hope. But when I arrived, he announced that God had finally spoken to him and demanded we confess our evil coupling without delay, including the news that I was with child. I begged him to wait a few more days. My mistress had just been convicted of murder. Even if she wished to beg mercy on my behalf, she no longer had the authority to demand it. I needed more time!" Her eyes were dulled with hopelessness. "I love the babe," she whispered.

Yet the maid was willing to let her mistress accept blame for a crime she did not commit, Eleanor thought, and felt harsh reason beginning to win the battle over her weaker woman's heart. It was not a victory she welcomed, but feared it was her only choice.

"I do not know why, but I told him it was too late anyway for a simple confession. I had killed Mistress Hursel because she was going to reveal that we had lain together. He stared at me in horrified silence. I shouted that I done so to keep our secret. Had it been discovered that I had quickened with child even before Mistress Hursel came, I would never have revealed he was the father and would have lied to protect him." Her sob was bereft of tears. "So I pleaded for him to look after me, as I had promised to shield him, and not reveal my crime against the butcher's widow until I had fled."

Eleanor was speechless.

"He leapt back from me with terror in his eyes and began to weep. It had been sinful enough to lie together, he cried, but now murder had been added to our wickedness. How much fouler would our souls grow if we delayed confession even a moment longer?"

The maid paused, as if hoping Eleanor would say something to make this agony cease, but the prioress could give little comfort.

"He turned to run back to the commandery and Father Pasche. I clutched at his sleeve, begging him not to do this. He was weeping but began to pull away, saying that God would not wait. We would soon be damned if we did not confess all. He was scared, as was I. I slipped and lost my grip on him."

Eleanor held her breath.

"I was desperate to stop him, but he was leaving me. I picked up a rock and struck him. He fell. When I bent over him, I knew he was dead." She stretched her hand out to Eleanor. "I never meant to kill, only to keep him from going to the priest. He was just a boy!"

Both of you were like children, terrified, and knew not where to turn, Eleanor thought. But what advice did she herself have at this moment? God was either remarkably silent or else she was unable to hear Him.

She took the maid's hand. The question was cruel but must be asked. "Did you drag his body to the pond and throw him in?"

Janeta jerked her hand away and stroked her belly. A blank expression washed over her face. "I do not know what I did, my lady. All I remember was arriving at the priory and finding Father Pasche and your monk in the garth."

A priest would take her confession now and speak of God's mercy, Eleanor thought, but Janeta must still suffer the penalty of secular law and hang.

"Now you know I have killed two people, yet I am with child. I know what will happen to me. Unlike my mistress, I cannot be granted mercy by the Prior of England for I have never taken vows. I must bear my child first and then be dragged to the gallows."

"There are other ways," the prioress said, desperately trying to find the words she needed. But they refused to come, and she felt as if she were wandering in some dark cave, begging for light but seeing none. The murder of the butcher's widow was deemed by many as just. Killing Brother Martin had been a tragic accident. Yet both were the result of yet another sin…

"No, my lady, there are none. If I had not killed Mistress Hursel, I still would have lost my child. Now I shall lose both the babe and my life."

"You must trust God's mercy," Eleanor said, and that, she believed with all her heart.

"God may forgive. In Him, I have great faith. It is men I do not trust."

As the prioress began to find a few of the words she needed to offer hope, Janeta forcibly pushed her away.

The last thing Eleanor remembered was the odd sensation of flight. Then her head struck the corner of the window, and everything went dark.

Chapter Thirty-seven

Sister Anne turned from the window, where she had been musing, and saw Janeta run down the corridor. The maid often did leave in a hurry, but the sub-infirmarian wondered what crucial errand Prioress Eleanor might have sent her on. Then she realized the door to the chamber was open and she felt uneasy. With no further hesitation, she hastened to the room.

Eleanor was lying on the floor.

In terror, Anne knelt beside her and bent to check her breath. Then her prioress groaned. Her arm rose to touch her forehead.

"I shall offer a gift for this blessing," Anne whispered to God and put her hand against the back of Eleanor's head. She felt a lump and a bit of blood, but nothing felt soft or broken.

Eleanor's eyes opened. "Where is she?"

Her eyes are unfocused, but her voice is strong, Anne thought with relief.

Eleanor struggled to sit up.

"Slowly!"

"Where is Janeta?"

"She has left but said nothing to me when she passed by. I assumed you had sent her on an errand. When I saw the open door, I came immediately." She frowned. "I should have stopped her, but I knew of no reason to do so." She braced Eleanor and helped her to sit back against the wall. "What has happened?"

"She killed both Mistress Hursel and Brother Martin. He was the father of her child. Mistress Hursel caught them lying together near the fishponds and threatened her with exposure if she did not pay her a fine price." Eleanor felt behind her and touched the stone wall. "I must have hit my head against that."

"Did she strike you?"

"I think she pushed me, but I'm not sure." Eleanor closed her eyes as if incredibly weary. "I was trying to find a way to give her hope and failed. She knows she must hang after giving birth to her child." She pressed a hand to her head and opened her eyes. With a look of uncertainty, Anne gazed at the door which remained open.

Other than the wind whistling as it struck the side of a window, there were no sounds from the hall.

"I don't know where Janeta fled, but we must catch her," Eleanor said. "I worry little about the safety of others, but fear most what she might do to herself. Had she wanted to kill me, she could have. Instead, she tried only to keep me from impeding her escape. I do not think she intended any real harm."

"You need care."

"Leave me and seek Brother Thomas, Father Pasche, and Brother Damian, who should send his men out on a search for her. Lest any of them think she is a frail woman, and thus no danger to them, you may tell them that she was strong enough to crack open Brother Martin's skull." Eleanor winced but had managed to stand with Anne's help. "If you can, please inform Prioress Emelyne of what has happened and then return to my side." She glanced at the wine. 'I swear to be obedient and do nothing until you are back."

"No wine," Anne said, jumping to her feet.

Then she ran out the door.

• • ● • •

The sub-infirmarian found Brother Damian just emerging with his sister from her audience chamber. Anne concisely explained what had happened.

Prioress Emelyne cried out in shock.

"It is imperative that we find Janeta as soon as possible," Anne said.

Damian nodded and said to his sister, "I will summon the brothers." Then he raced toward the men's house.

"What can I do?" Prioress Emelyne rested a hand on the nun's arm.

"Send Sister Richolda to tend Prioress Eleanor until I return. I could not examine her properly before she ordered me to seek you and others to find Janeta."

The prioress summoned a nun.

With a few words of thanks, the sub-infirmarian left to follow Brother Damian.

● ● ● ● ●

Brother Thomas was walking with a grim-faced Father Pasche toward the nuns' priory when they saw Brother Damian running toward them with Sister Anne not far behind.

"I pray that there has not been another murder," Thomas said to the priest.

Damian was clutching his stump. "We must find Janeta," he panted. "She confessed to Prioress Eleanor that she had killed both Mistress Hursel and Brother Martin, and then she struck the prioress and fled. Have you seen her coming this way?"

"We have not," Father Pasche replied.

"Has our prioress been seriously hurt?" Thomas felt an icy hand grip his heart.

The commander had turned away and was looking around frantically.

Thomas almost grabbed Damian in anger for not answering his question but drew back. "Our prioress?" he repeated, hissing through his teeth.

"She is well enough," Anne replied as she joined the men. "A bump on the head. But she wants Janeta caught. She said she is less danger to others than to herself."

"Why does she think that?" Father Pasche asked, inexplicably raising a thoughtful finger to his cheek as if he were about to engage them all in debate.

This did nothing to assuage Thomas' brittle temper. "She is never wrong," he snapped, glaring at the two men. "Where would the maid go? Friends? Family in the village or nearby?" "None," Damian said. "She came with her mistress and spent all her time at her side."

"She was pregnant," Sister Anne said, and then added, "Brother Martin was the father."

The priest stared at her in disbelief. Brother Damian's mouth dropped open.

"This is not the time to explain or ponder these details," she said. "It is imperative that we find her. Now!"

Thomas gazed down the path to the preceptory, and next at the one leading to the fishponds. Had the maid run toward the village or, ignoring both the dangers of outlaws and sheriff's men searching for her, chosen roads leading away from it? Had she been so terrified that she believed it possible to escape to some distant city or even to the coast where a fisherman might take her to Wales for the price of her body? Was there any reason, no matter how irrational, for her to go in any particular direction?

He felt powerless. He did not know this land, and he did not know the maid.

Then an idea struck him. "Where did Janeta and Brother Martin meet to lie together?"

"The fishponds," Anne replied. Reading his intent, she added, "If you were outside the commandery for any time, you would have seen her had she come this way."

"What other ways, besides this path, are there to reach the ponds?" Thomas looked at the two men. "I fear she may have gone there to commit self-murder."

As if awakening from a bad dream, the priest blinked. "Follow me," he said and set off back to the preceptory.

• • ● • •

It took little time to reach the dirt path that broke away from the road just outside the walls of Mynchen Buckland Priory and led to the ponds.

The water had overflowed the banks in several places and washed away some of the path. Roots from the willows were even more exposed than usual. Here and there, they saw footprints in the soft mud. Because the maid was taller than many women, and thus had larger feet, none of them could say if the tracks were hers or those of a man from the village who might have hoped to net a few fish the night before.

Brother Thomas spotted one place where the earth had recently crumbled and collapsed into the pond. But the ground was not as muddy there, and he could not determine if any marks seen were from footprints.

No one could see any sign of the maid, nor did they spy a body.

Brother Damian sent for a lay brother and a rope.

When he arrived, the man flushed with embarrassment as he glanced at Sister Anne. She turned her back, and he stripped, tied the rope around his waist, and jumped into the water. Brother Thomas held fast to the rope end so he could drag the man to safety if he floundered in the mud and pond weeds.

Normally, the depth would have been only a couple of feet to allow for easy fishing, but the rains had swollen the ponds significantly. According to Brother Damian, the swifter currents from the melting snows had also hollowed out dangerous holes in the bed of the pond. A man could slip into one and drown if he could not swim.

"We can send a lay brother to the island in a boat if needed," Brother Damian said, "but I doubt she could have reached it by now."

"Could she swim?" Father Pasche asked.

No one knew.

Did she even come this way? Thomas asked himself, yet he felt certain she had. If Janeta had fled without any destination in mind, her sorrow might well have driven her first to the one place she had found a brief joy—or else her guilt required she die where she had killed the father of her child.

• • ● • •

It was a long time before the man found Janeta.

She was dead. The long weeds had already wrapped around her body and neck yet only gently held her below the surface.

When they dragged her out, Brother Thomas immediately knelt by the body to whisper God's comfort in the maid's cold ear and offer a plea that He grant her mercy.

But had she died by accident or intent?

Both Father Pasche and Brother Damian wanted to know and turned to the sub-infirmarian for her opinion.

Brother Thomas and Sister Anne first examined the area where the girl had fallen in. The rim of the pond had collapsed, dragging some of the path with it. To keep further erosion from occurring, rocks had been placed to brace the dirt, but several of those had fallen into the water. A small exposed tree root arched above ground near the outside edge of the narrowed walkway.

"This seems to have been recently pulled up," Thomas said to Anne and leaned down to wiggle the willow root. The ground on either side of the exposed root was loosened, and the earth was still damp.

Sister Anne nodded, then turned back to kneel by the corpse. She examined the maid's body and struggled not to weep when she put a hand on the dead woman's belly. How could she prove that this death was not a sin? Despite the two murders this maid had committed, and perhaps against all reason, Anne still did not want to add another transgression to weigh down Janeta's soul.

But when she turned Janeta's head to examine the other side, she knew that her prayer had been answered. There was a large gash on the woman's forehead.

Anne stood up and studied the angle of the exposed root and glanced at where the rock-lined pond bank was. In her blind rush, Janeta must have tripped on the root which would have sent her tumbling headfirst against the stones lining the rim of the pond. The blow would not have been hard enough to kill, but it was probably enough to have stunned the maid. If so, she would have been unconscious when she fell into the pond. It would have been easy to drown under those circumstances.

The sub-infirmarian looked up at the men. "There is no evidence of self-murder," she said. "Janeta may have been guilty of other grave crimes, but she did not commit this one."

Chapter Thirty-eight

Immediately after the morning Office, Prioress Eleanor followed the three Hospitallers into the cell. The door was unlocked, and the brightness of wax candles shone from within. The elderly lay brother had been replaced with a round-cheeked, older nun who now served the former prisoner.

They were met by a silent Amicia standing before the small altar where she had spent so many hours praying in the dark. No longer did she bear the appearance of a convicted and contrite murderer. Instead, she faced them with the quiet dignity of one who was accustomed to leading God's servants with justice, wisdom, and piety. Her face was somber. Her hands were clasped and held close to her waist.

Discreetly taking a place to the rear of the party, Eleanor looked around at the still plain but more cheerful room. But now there was also an odd dusty scent in the air which she had never noticed before. With deep sadness, she wondered if the earth had already begun to claim the body of this woman long promised by Death.

Prioress Emelyne dropped to her knees. "My lady, you are free. All charges have been dropped. You were wrongly condemned for a transgression you did not commit."

Without saying a word, Amicia gazed over the head of the kneeling woman at the two men standing behind. Her look expressed a simple question.

Father Pasche and Brother Damian quickly knelt as well.

"It was Janeta, your maid, who killed both Mistress Hursel and Brother Martin," Emelyne continued and briefly explained the reasons for the crimes. "She has since died."

Not a muscle moved in Amicia's face, but Eleanor noticed that her eyes had closed for just an instant longer than the usual blink.

"After confessing to Prioress Eleanor, Janeta escaped and ran to the fishponds. The ground caved in, and she drowned." Emelyne began to stumble over her words. "Brother Thomas whispered forgiveness in her ear."

Amicia said nothing.

Eleanor concluded that the woman's silence was unnerving the trio. The two men had begun to twitch.

Emelyne reached out with hands clenched together as if begging for mercy from a vengeful angel. "She was never tried for her crimes," she said softly, "nor, according to Sister Anne of Tyndal Priory, is the manner of her death an obvious sin. We three have discussed begging the Prior of England for permission to bury her honorably so she may rise with others on the Judgment Day." She waited for a reaction from the intimidating woman. If she had thought to gain some favor by this means, none was forthcoming.

"You may beg if you so desire. That is your right," Amicia said in a calm voice, "but I shall not join in your plea. She was an unrepentant murderer. Whether or not she was tried, she admitted the crimes."

Eleanor noticed that Amicia's jaw was tensed, but not, she realized, with anger. This was iron self-control from a dying woman determined to survive this ordeal. Discreetly, she bowed her head in respect.

Swallowing her surprise over Amicia's reply, Prioress Emelyne folded her hands more prayerfully and lowered her eyes with deep humility. "My lady, I have grievously sinned against you. Before I speak these words in Chapter, I must confess to you first. Overwhelmed as I was with wicked ambition to take your place as prioress here, I listened to evil counsel and willingly acted to unjustly depose you. I shut my ears to the weak arguments supporting your guilt and ignored the obvious truth that you were incapable of the crime." She looked up at Amicia as if again seeking approval. The woman remained silent. Only her eyes revealed a mix of sadness and desire to listen with compassion.

"With joy, I greet the news that your innocence has been proven, and therefore I now resign the position I stole from you, return the seal of office to your rightful possession, and ask that my crime be reported to the Prior of England." She reached into her robe and pulled out a rolled parchment. "In this letter to him, I have summarized my transgressions. Until he renders his verdict, I will accept any punishment you deem appropriate."

Amicia accepted the parchment and quickly read it. Placing it on the small table beside her, she said, "I accept your resignation and your desire to confess to our Prior in Clerkenwell. The letter will be sent to him by special messenger this day." Briefly, she leaned on the table. "As for accepting the position of prioress, I shall do so, but only until such time as the nuns in Chapter are able to elect another in my place. As you all know, my health is rapidly failing, and I beg all that this election take place mercifully soon. Mynchen Buckland and the men's commandery need stable leadership, and our work to fund the charity done by the Order in Outremer must continue with no further interruption."

Emelyne slumped as if bone weary and struck with melancholy.

Eleanor wondered if the cause was shame and guilt, relief that her confession was over, or due to her loss of any hope that her sins would remain hidden.

"Henceforth, you shall be Sister Emelyne and dwell with the other nuns, those who hold no office in this priory, until such time as our Prior renders his verdict in your case. When he does so, we shall all honor his decision, whatever that might be. For my part, I willingly forgive any offense you may have committed against me and beg you to forgive any of mine against you."

Emelyne murmured assent.

Prioress Amicia gestured for the chastised woman to rise and stand apart. Then she looked to her right and nodded at Father Pasche. "You have much to say to me as well."

"I, too, have sinned against you, my lady, by falling victim to the Devil's trickery. In the guise of Mistress Hursel, a wicked woman, he whispered vile rumors about you before you took vows. Although I distrusted them at the time they were reported to me, the rot infected my soul. When I saw you with blood on your hands, the festering tainted my judgment. On no evidence, I concluded you had escaped all punishment for one unproven crime, that this second showed a pattern of evil, and I was determined that you suffer for this latest." Tears were coming down his cheeks. "My arguments for your guilt at the Chapter trial were spoken by Satan through my lips and using my tongue. I beg forgiveness and will accept any punishment you exact."

"Stand up, Father," Prioress Amicia said. "I freely give forgiveness. In my confinement, you offered consolation. In the pain of my ill-health, you brought balm to my soul. If you sinned, it was because you suffered a failure of reason, one that I sinfully abetted. The nuns also came to the same conclusion about my guilt and may well have done so even if you had not said what you did. We are all flawed creatures, a fact we often forget in our worldly arrogance. So I feel no malice toward you and ask no penance other than what your own confessor orders. You have told me why you argued as you did, begged my forgiveness, and that is sufficient to me." She gestured for him to step aside.

Brother Damian leapt to his feet, holding his stump and grimacing with pain. "You know my sin, Prioress Amicia, as does my sister. Before we knew of Janeta's guilt, I confessed it all to the now Sister Emelyne, thus I need not speak of it again." Looking over his shoulder, he glowered at Prioress Eleanor just behind him. "Especially in public."

Eleanor raised an eyebrow but said nothing.

With an expression of disgust, Sister Emelyne watched her elder sibling bluster.

Spinning around, he pointed at Prioress Amicia. "You toler-
ated it," he said to her and shook his finger.
She remained utterly still for a long time
Sweat beaded on his forehead. His hand fell to his side.
Finally, she answered. "You are a wrathful, arrogant man,
Brother Damian, but you are also as weak as frayed cloth. Yes, I
tolerated your embezzlement of priory funds for a time. In that,
I bear great blame. But lest you think no one else knew of your
cowardice in Outremer, I must now tell you that my husband
told many others of it, not just Mistress Hursel, when he drank
too much at table. He even boasted to me of how swiftly he cut
off your hand."
Damian cried out in agony and collapsed on the floor.
Father Pasche rushed to his side, but the man waved him
away and began to weep.
"Yet I knew that your wound caused you much agony and
believed that was penance enough for fleeing battle. It was weak
of me, but I also grieved that you, or anyone, should fall victim
to my husband and Mistress Hursel who were creatures much
beloved by the Prince of Darkness. For that, I erred in judgment
and chose to hide your theft."
Damian gripped his stump and whimpered.
Eleanor wondered if his cries were due less to the pain in his
arm and more to the realization than everyone now knew about
his crime against the Order and his personal shame.
"As I must soon face God, I shall forgive all your sins against
me. What is not mine to forgive is your willingness to let any
innocent person be found guilty so your own sins might remain
hidden."
He waved piteously at her, begging to be heard.
"I do not wish to hear your feeble excuses, Brother. Had
another stood in my place, knowing what I did about your shame
and guilt, I believe that you would have found some cruel way
to silence him."
"Not murder!" he howled.

"Only your soul and God know that." She placed her hand on a document that lay next to Prioress Emelyne's confession. "Nor have I the right to forgive you for stealing from the Order and denying our hospitals all the funds needed to heal the sick. I have therefore written the details of your theft to our Prior and fully explained my reasons and part in hiding it. Both these messages will be sent this day to Clerkenwell."

"Please, my lady! No! I plead for clemency!" Tears flooded his cheeks, and he banged his head on the floor.

"You received leniency a long time ago, Brother Damian, and abused the charity," she replied. "Father Pasche?"

The priest stepped forward.

"Take this man back to his chamber in the commandery. Lock the door and set a guard. That shall become his prison until the Prior renders his verdict. But treat him kindly and allow Sister Richolda to provide him with the medicine required to ease the pain of his physical wound." Sadness briefly flickered in her eyes. "I know you will do all you can to treat his spiritual ones."

Firmly but gently, the priest pulled Brother Damian to his feet and pushed him out the door.

Prioress Amicia gave Sister Emelyne permission to follow and give comfort to her distraught brother, if she so desired.

Then she looked at Prioress Eleanor. "If you will, please shut the door," she said a voice that was suddenly humble and slightly pleading. "I beg that you remain alone with me for just a short while longer. Although I know you will begin your journey back to your priory today, it would be a kindness. There is something I must tell you."

"Of course," Eleanor replied, a bit perplexed. After all that had happened and been said in these tragic matters, she could not imagine what more there could possibly be left to tell.

Chapter Thirty-nine

When Eleanor turned around after shutting the door, she saw that Prioress Amicia was now seated on her cot.

"Please join me here," she said. Her demeanor had softened, her smile was warm, but profound weariness had finally conquered her ability to hide frailty. "I no longer have the strength to stand, and looking up wearies me beyond endurance."

As she sat beside her, Eleanor reached out for the woman's hand. It was dry as parchment and cold as stone. Death stands very near to her indeed, she thought, and begged God to be gentle in those hours when the woman's soul struggled for release.

"I will keep my promise not to delay your departure, but I have a confession to make that only you and God must hear in this place."

Eleanor nodded. In ways, Prioress Amicia reminded her of her dead aunt, Sister Beatrice, and that calmed her. Yet she knew her guilt over failing to save Janeta and the lost babe were only set aside and would return to haunt her soon enough.

"I know you wonder why I refused to declare my innocence until you came to speak with me. On my deathbed, I would have confessed my innocence. But when I was accused and saw the expression on Janeta's face, I knew she had killed Mistress Hursel. I had already suspected she was with child. And thus I allowed the blame to be placed on me. I am dying and wicked enough. In that instant, I decided my soul could not be any darker if it had one more festering sin, and that lie was a little enough transgression."

"You would have let her escape all consequences for her crimes?" Eleanor said this in a sharp tone, then realized her words betrayed a rigid arrogance born out of her own failures and had little to do with Janeta's sins. "Forgive me for those harsh words. I want to understand and have no right to condemn."

Amicia dismissed the need for apology. "You think she would have suffered no consequences for killing Mistress Hursel? Let me ask you this. What can a young woman of her rank do with a bastard child at her breast but without kin or mistress? Beg in the streets?"

"For a woman that usually leads to whoring."

"And to some that is a fouler sin than lying once with a man, even one who has sworn to be chaste." Her eyes shut for an instant. "And her babe? The Hospitallers might well have taken it to raise, but she would never have seen her child again. That is a grief far more painful than this canker that will soon kill me."

"But she killed Brother Martin."

"And I blame myself for that. Had I spoken to Prioress Emelyne earlier about offering the security of a place here, even though Janeta would have had to surrender her child, that death would have been avoided. And if I had spoken frankly with Janeta as well…" Her voice trembled.

Eleanor knew she was struggling with her next words.

"As you heard me say earlier, Janeta is a murderer and, perhaps, an unrepentant one. Yet I confess I might have forgiven her for the death of Mistress Hursel, as many others did in fact. That is a mortal's selfish rationale, for we must ask if anyone but God has the right to kill another, even justly."

"I share your doubts."

"As for the death of the young lay brother? When my guard was dismissed, and I first learned of Brother Martin's death and cause, I had neither reason nor right to forgive that crime. Yet I do take the sin of Brother Martin's murder on myself as well because my ill-conceived decisions and failure to properly guide led to it. I shall add that transgression to my deathbed confession."

As Amicia caught her breath, Eleanor felt something far more chilling was coming.

"By now, you have heard the rumor that I killed my husband?"

"I have." Eleanor's voice did not betray her unease.

"The story is true."

Amicia nodded at their joined hands. "You did not withdraw your hand, and your eyes do not condemn me," she said. "You continue to listen, yet have not rendered judgment."

"Truth is rarely as simple as men claim," Eleanor replied. "I cannot swear that I will not judge, only that I will hear, with an open heart, all you have to say in this matter."

"My husband and I never found joy in each other. I gave him no children. He gave me little courtesy. As men, whether good or evil, often do, he found other women to bed, mostly servants, yet did not even father bastards for me to raise. When he could, he went to war. When he could not, he reveled in wine." She rubbed her fingers under her eyes.

Eleanor saw no hint of tears.

"After too many cups, he became violent and, for my barrenness, would sometimes beat me." She looked away. "Out of mercy, some of his men took pity on me and tried, most nights, to lead him to a whore or a bed where he usually fell asleep. But one evening, after he had returned from Outremer, he escaped his fellows and sought me out, dragging me from my bed by my hair. At the top of the stairs, he pulled me to my feet, then struck me until I bled and earned this scar where his ring cut my lips."

"Dear God," Eleanor whispered.

Amicia's voice dropped to a whisper, her gaze becoming distant as if seeing it all again. "I don't know why he released me. He was screaming and then lunged at me. I stepped aside." She took her hand from Eleanor's and pointed to the left. "He fell, headfirst, down the stairs." She gestured downward, her expressionless eyes staring. "It was so silent. His body lay awkwardly at the bottom of the stone steps. I knew he was dead."

She glanced at Eleanor as if still amazed by what had happened.

Neither said a word.

Tears slipped down her cheeks. "Even now," Amicia murmured, "I avoid the whole truth. As he fell, his hand reached out. I stepped away. Had I taken his hand, perhaps his fall would have been broken and my husband might have lived. But I denied him that mercy, and thus I am guilty of his death."

"He might not have lived, or more likely taken you to your own death with him," Eleanor replied.

"I did not even try," Amicia said. "For that, I own guilt."

Eleanor could not so easily condemn, although she was beginning to understand why Amicia had been inclined to forgive Janeta for the murder of the butcher's widow. "Did Mistress Hursel witness this?"

"She saw the corpse, looked up, and observed me standing there. When the sheriff arrived, my husband's guests that night said he had drunk deeply, as was his custom, and brought no blame on me. Indeed, his very sweat stank of wine. One swore he had seen me come late to the staircase and vouched for my horror and grief at the sight of the corpse."

Eleanor nodded. Out of sympathy, those who knew how brutally a husband beat his wife often did their best to protect her from any suspicion should he fall victim to a questionable accident.

"Mistress Hursel later asked for money to keep her silence. I told her that she had no proof and dismissed her from my service. As for Janeta, she saw nothing that night but later bathed my wounds with kind gentleness." Amicia put one hand on her breast. "I confessed my sins to my priest, a man who chose mercy, and then I begged the Prior of England to let me take vows. Soon after, I donned this shirt of thorns in penance for killing my husband."

"Father Pasche was here when you arrived."

"We have never spoken of his brother's death, yet I realized during my trial that he must have heard the rumors when he spoke so fiercely against me. But he was kind to me after my conviction, and I do not blame him for concluding I could have killed Mistress Hursel if I had also murdered his brother."

"And because you believe you are guilty of your husband's death, yet you had found a priest who offered forgiveness, you were willing to excuse Janeta's murder of Mistress Hursel?"

"Mistress Hursel lived in the Devil's heart. She could not destroy me. Of what value is the word of a servant when men of rank swear she is wrong? As for Brother Damian, he is a weak and craven man, yet my husband had already delivered to him a savage justice for his cowardice. What right had Mistress Hursel to extort money when he had paid the price for his transgression? And she has done far more to others. I could not see Janeta condemned for sending this woman's soul back to Hell."

Eleanor wanted to argue but was not up to the debate. Janeta was dead. Her soul was facing God. Whether or not she was satisfied with Prioress Amicia's logic, she believed there would be justice in accordance with God's law for both Janeta and the butcher's widow.

Her thoughts were interrupted as she felt Amicia press something into her hand. She looked at her palm and saw the ring Sister Anne had found in the garth.

"In time, and if you deem the circumstances right, I beg you to give this ring to your nephew, Richard FitzHugh. When you do, and only if you feel it wise, tell him that his mother never ceased to love him and that I begged God, with my last breath, to guide and protect him."

Chapter Forty

Eleanor was speechless.

The dying woman gently closed her companion's hand over the ring. "Your brother gave me that ring when our son was born. May God forgive me, but I have never repented the gift or the reason it was given."

This, Eleanor thought, is why you forgave Janeta so much. You understood what she must face when she was forced to surrender her child.

"Your brother is a kind man. He saw my wounds and learned how my husband beat me. Indeed, when he visited us, he tried to protect me from the blows. After my husband left to fight the Infidel, Hugh's comfort and my longing for it led us to bed many times. When I quickened with child, he promised to send me to a remote manor house where I might give birth in secret. The women in attendance were skilled and gentle. Your brother was present and welcomed the babe with joy."

"He has never spoken of this."

She smiled. "Yet he has raised Richard as if he had been born of a lawful marriage and regularly sent me news. Not long ago, he told me that Richard had chosen to serve the king in matters of the law."

"I had hoped he would become a priest," Eleanor replied. "I confess it."

"A man can serve God without taking vows and serve his king without taking up a sword." Looking at her companion's expression, she laughed but the sound was far weaker than it had been. "Yes, he told me how you and he had argued over that. I praised your wisdom in suggesting the boy go to Oxford and choose his own way."

"I did not even know your name," Eleanor said quietly as she carefully stored the ring in her pouch.

Prioress Amicia suddenly bent forward and groaned.

Eleanor hugged her gently and comforted her. "You are weary," she said, feeling each bone in Amicia's body through the thin flesh that barely covered them.

"And shall die very soon," the woman said and forced herself to sit up once again. "I have but little more to say, and then you must leave."

Eleanor told Amicia that she regretted she had not met her until now, yet appreciated why Hugh had kept the secret.

"And I kept one from him. Only this one. The reason my husband beat me with such severity the night he died is because he had learned of my adultery. He did not know of the child I bore. Had he, he might well have killed me. But I knew who must have told him about my infidelity, and I have struggled to banish my hatred for Mistress Hursel. Will you swear never to tell your brother that? He would not forgive himself for the harm done to me, and he owns no fault in what happened that night."

Although she wished it could be otherwise, Eleanor gave her oath to remain silent.

"After my husband's death, your brother wished to marry me so we could raise our son together. I refused, confessing my crime that caused my husband's death. I said I must take vows to atone. He grieved over my decision but understood."

And none of us knew any of this, Eleanor thought. Or did our father? She doubted it. Perhaps Hugh would have told him if Amicia had agreed to marriage.

"Not long ago, I sent him word that I was dying. His reply was the letter you brought. In it, he said he was going to fight the Welsh under our king and might die as well. He begged me to tell you the truth of our son's birth so you might decide whether to tell Richard the story, how much to tell, or when. Someone must know it, he said, and you were the one person he trusted without question to make the right decisions."

Eleanor swallowed stinging tears.

"When I read his letter, I knew I could not die, convicted of a murder I did not commit. That my son might someday learn that his mother, had she not taken vows and died of this canker, would have been hanged was more than I could bear."

Struggling to keep her emotions in control, Eleanor simply nodded.

"I knew the evidence against me was weak. If only I had responded with the outrage of an innocent woman, Father Pasche would not have set himself against me, and the others concurred for their own reasons. Instead, I suggested guilt by my refusal to say I had done nothing. I only prayed that you expose the conviction as inadequate and inform the Prior of England. As for Janeta, I knew it was unlikely that her guilt would be found out. What evidence was there that pointed to anyone?" She gazed sadly at Eleanor. "I was aware of your reputation but should have known better than to assume you would not uncover the whole truth."

There was too much to say, and no time left to say it. The two women looked at each other with mutual affection. If they had differences of opinion, they would have an eternity to debate them once their souls met again. For now, neither had any desire to do so.

Eleanor broke the silence first. "I have grown confident that your son will become a fine counselor to our king," she said, "now that God has allowed me to meet his most remarkable mother."

"And I believe it as well, for I have met his most exceptional aunt." Prioress Amicia bowed her head.

Eleanor knew it was time to depart. She stood.

Prioress Amicia forced herself to rise as well. "Grant me your blessing," she said, "for I must soon stand before the terrible face of God. I swear to you that I shall confess all evil of which I am guilty and hope for mercy in those transgressions I am too blinded by sin to acknowledge. Your blessing would give me courage to accept His sentence."

Without hesitation, Eleanor gave it, then took the dying woman into her arms and kissed her on both cheeks.

With an expression warm with gratitude, Prioress Amicia gently rested her fingers on the arm of her son's aunt, and then turned away to face the small altar.

Prioress Eleanor left the small room without speaking and closed the door. Although she longed to do so, she did not look back at this woman whom she would never again see in this world.

• • ● • •

Not long after, the trio of monastics, surrounded by their armed guard, began their long journey home to Tyndal Priory. When Mynchen Buckland Priory had faded deep into the mists of Somerset, their sadness over the tragic events at the priory also began to dull. The sun may have failed to shine for days, but spirits slowly rose.

They did for all, that is, except Prioress Eleanor. She smiled with courtesy but no mirth when Brother Thomas tried to distract her with a witty tale. Even Sister Anne found her friend uncommonly distant.

Eleanor knew that she, too, would eventually tuck her grief over all the events at the Hospitaller priory deep into her heart and laugh again with honest ease. But she also feared she might never forgive herself for solving the crimes but failing to find the balm needed to heal the fear and sorrows of Janeta, the maid.

Author's Notes

When I introduced Hugh's illegitimate son, Richard, in *Tyrant of the Mind*, I had not yet become acquainted with the boy's mother. After I brought Richard back as a teenager in *Land of Shadows*, however, she rather insistently tapped my shoulder. Wasn't it finally time for us to get to know each other? I'm so glad we did. Sadly, I only met her at the end of her life but found her quite fascinating as well as complex, although certainly not without faults. In this tale, she also graciously allowed me to introduce the Order of the Hospital of Saint John of Jerusalem, commonly called the Hospitallers. For that, I owe her special thanks, as authors must with the surprising gifts their characters always seem to bring.

The Templars have become very popular, especially in fiction, while the Hospitallers have gotten shorter shrift. That is undeserved.

Unlike other military Orders, the Hospitallers have survived in various forms to the present time. As an example, the non-denominational St. John Ambulance Brigade is one particularly famous descendant. After the Hospitallers left Acre for Rhodes and Malta, they showed remarkable ability to adapt. When soldiers became less important, the Order built both commercial vessels and a naval fleet. Eventually, they also shifted away from their militaristic role and back to their original charitable roots.

There is so much I should write about the history of this Order, both in the Medieval era and beyond, but that would require more than any author can do in short notes. In my usual bibliography at the end, I have listed a number of fascinating volumes of various lengths and detail by scholars. Many include illustrations, photographs, and archaeological details. These should satisfy curiosity, no matter what the specific interest.

Therefore, I shall be brief here, and, instead of discussing the military and hierarchical parts of the Order, I will concentrate on the lesser-known, original purpose: charity to all the poor and disadvantaged as well their remarkable medical work. I confess that this decision is also a bit personal. In this troubled era of ours, I find the enlightened work done by a Medieval Order, at a time many view as far more ignorant and violent than our own, to be rather heartening.

The Order developed from a hospital already in Jerusalem when the city was captured by Christians in 1099. The date this institution was originally founded is unclear, but it was run by a small group of monks, possibly lay brothers, from a nearby abbey. The Order itself began sometime before 1113 when these brothers broke away from their specific abbey. Their leader, Gerald, origins unknown, is acknowledged as the first Master of what formally became the Order of the Hospital of Saint John of Jerusalem.

Although emphasis on caring for the poor has always been a stated Christian principle, the unique dedication of the Hospitallers to this mission, from the time of Gerald, presages the movement later founded by St Francis of Assisi. The Hospitaller devotion was so profound they referred to themselves as the "serfs of the poor" and made no distinction if the individual in need was male, female, orphan, Christian, Jewish, or Muslim. Such inclusive charity was unusual.

The increasing number of pilgrims to the sacred sites in Outremer made medical and charitable care an obvious need. Not only was any travel long and arduous, but the unstable political situation and religious quarrels (of several varieties) added to the dangers. Many of the pilgrims were poor, sick, or became so in the course of their journey due to unfamiliar diseases, debilitation, attacks, robberies, or unexpected expenses and exorbitant prices charged by the usual commercial predators. If they made it in one piece to Jerusalem, and later Acre, they were lucky indeed. If they were sick or impoverished, they could turn to the Hospitallers.

The Jerusalem and Acre hospitals may have been different in size, but the method and quality of care was the same. Other than lepers, cared for at other hospitals in the cities, all were welcomed. Men and women were segregated. There was a specific maternity ward as well as one for critical cases. If the number of sick exceeded the beds, the attending brothers gave up their own and slept on the floors. Hospitaller servants went out into the city to bring in those too sick to make it to the hospital. A portable tent, staffed with surgeons and other medical personnel, was taken to battles for the care of the wounded, and if these needed additional care, they were transported to the closest hospital in an early form of an ambulance service. All Hospitallers, including brother knights, were required to give up their horses and walk if the sick needed the animals for transportation.

The care given was incredibly expensive even for the time. The sick had individual beds with feather mattresses and a diet rich in fresh meat, fruits, and vegetables. There was a separate kitchen for those with digestive problems, and provision was made for the patients with other dietary restrictions such as Jews and Muslims. If a patient required help getting to the latrine, there was a servant to assist, as well as one to change sheets every two weeks, bathe the patient, and even remove calluses with a pumice stone after feet were washed in hot water.

Needless to say, this explains why the main purpose of Hospitaller priories outside of Outremer was to manage their properties well so a great deal of money could be sent to the hospital work in Outremer. A much smaller portion was required by the brother knights and brother sergeants for battle costs.

From our point of view, the physicians, in specific, were few in number. Only four served in Jerusalem, a hospital that had the capacity to house two thousand patients. They were also, not surprisingly, Christian. That said, the Order welcomed medical caregivers from other faiths if their expertise was required in special situations or emergencies when the hospital had more patients than usual. Muslim doctors, for instance, were renowned for eye care.

Although there is some debate about how much Hospitaller care was influenced by the expertise found amongst local Jewish and Muslim practitioners, there is a strong suggestion that doctors have always been doctors and thus shared knowledge because they cared about improving treatment. Standard medical practices seem to have been based on the medical school teachings at Salerno that emphasized cleanliness, good diet, rest, and attentive nursing.

As one last comment about general Hospitaller care in Outremer, I will mention a bit about their charitable work with women and children. If they discovered a woman in the city too poor to clothe her children, they sent alms and clothing. If the mother was too sick to care for her children, they arranged for substitute care. In the maternity ward, a small cot was placed next to the new mother so the baby would be close by. Female servants cared for the new mothers, washed the baby after birth, and wet-nurses were provided for those who could not nurse themselves. If a mother was forced to abandon her baby, for whatever reason, the Order had an orphanage to raise the child, teach him or her a useful skill, and give them all the choice, at a suitable age, to remain with the Order or go out into the world.

Since the Hospitaller Order was service-oriented, unlike the contemplative Benedictines, they observed the more flexible Rule of St. Augustine in order to accommodate the needs of their hospital and charity work within the community. Contact with the secular world by both genders was common, and, as a consequence, their strict adherence to the vow of chastity was often questioned. Unlike other Orders, Hospitaller nuns and brothers were allowed to own a few personal items, but horses and armor were retained by the Order when the brother knight using them died.

Unlike other military Orders, women seemed to have always been very welcomed by the Hospitallers. They usually joined because they had brother knights as family members and were therefore of aristocratic birth. This meant they brought lands or rents with them to the Order and had wealthy friends and family who were inclined to donate. Some women may also have been drawn by the charitable element.

Brothers and nuns were housed separately. Often, the women were under the control of the male prior, also known as a commander. Sometimes the prioress, who was elected by her nuns, controlled the finances of her own house. Occasionally, the prioress was also called a commander, like her male counterpart in the Order, but this was rare. All Hospitaller houses in England were under the rule of the Prior of England in Clerkenwell, who was responsible for discipline, collecting priory tithes, approval of elections, and providing spiritual as well as temporal guidance. In cases where a religious was convicted of some offense in the local priory Chapter, the Prior of England had the right, especially in serious offenses, to determine punishment.

There is very little documentation discussing the role of women in hospital care. Brothers were in charge of the wards in Outremer, but male and female paid servants tended the patients. Servants of both genders made beds, washed patients, and cooked, although men and women were segregated so it might be plausibly assumed that men cared for men, and women for women. Since conventional wisdom stated that women provided the best care of children, however, it is thought that the maternity ward and orphanage were under the supervision of a woman. Rather than a paid servant, this may have been a lay or, much less likely, a professed sister. In the case of Sister Richolda, I thought it realistic to make her a servant in Acre and to assume that midwives, not doctors, regularly treated birthing mothers.

The Mynchen Buckland Priory (also called a preceptory) in my story was a real place. The location rests in a small valley in Somerset at Lower Durston. Although the buildings no longer exist, vague earthworks remain, part of the wall of a barn, an unattached stone window, and much of the large fishpond area with small islands. The main buildings, as Brother Thomas notes, were on high ground. A small priory or commandery of brothers was placed next door.

The main priory originally belonged to a group of Augustinian canons, but, in approximately 1185, they were removed and the property given to the Hospitallers to establish a centralized priory for their English nuns. This was done by King Henry II, a man who seems to have had his hand in everything, and the given reason for the eviction of the canons sounds very similar to why the Benedictine nuns were removed from Amesbury Priory so the Order of Fontevraud could move in: bad behavior on the part of the original resident religious. In both instances, the alleged sins of the displaced have not been convincingly well-documented.

In short order, all Hospitaller nuns in England were moved to Mynchen Buckland. From an administrative viewpoint, this made sense because most commanderies had very few nuns, and these were surrounded by a much larger number of brothers. From a religious standpoint, it satisfied a Church that was growing ever more uncomfortable with the temptations men faced when women, albeit religious ones, were too close by.

By 1338, there were fifty nuns in residence at Mynchen Buckland and six brothers. Since I have no information on how many were there in 1282, I made the assumption that the number of both would be even fewer. There were documented and ongoing tensions between the nuns and brothers. The brothers resented having to pay for the chaplains who served the nuns as well as their shared steward. The nuns argued, with documented justification, that they did not have enough income to pay for their own expenses as it was. In any case, all commanderies had to send a portion of their income to the Prior of England to fund the costs of the Order overseas. That the fictional Brother Damian was taking a little cream off the top would have been a serious offense.

I must apologize to the Medieval Order for making the Mynchen Buckland religious community the scene of murders and presenting some of the members as less than admirable suspects. Doing so is the curse of the mystery writer and in no way reflects my opinion of the Hospitallers. Their Medieval history is impressive, and their charitable work was commendable. Although I wish Sister Richolda had existed, none of the members of the monastic community in my story ever did. In 1280, the real prioress was Alienor de Actune, but the next name does not occur until 1292. Since I do not know whether Alienor de Actune was prioress until 1292, or there were others unnamed during those years, I took license and inserted Amicia and Emelyne. In the men's house, the preceptor or commander in 1281 was Richard de Brampford with the next name mentioned in 1321. Again, I inserted Damian, and hope I have not insulted history too much.

Bibliography

The following are books which I found informative and fascinating on Hospitaller history in general and the priory at Mynchen Buckland in specific. I would also like to give special thanks to the Taunton Visitor Centre who referred me to the Somerset Heritage Centre. The archivist, Graeme Edwards, at the Heritage Centre provided me with a link to their online maps, dating from the nineteenth century, and other data which provided invaluable information about the area around the old priory. It is also thanks to Mr. Edwards that I did not make a terrible geographical mistake and move a stream to a place it never existed!

Women in the Military Orders of the Crusades, by Myra Miranda Bom; Palgrave Macmillan, 2012.

The Hospitallers, the Mediterranean and Europe (Festschrift for Anthony Luttrell), edited by Karl Borchardt, Nikolas Jaspert, and Helen J. Nicholson; Ashgate, 2007.

The History of Mynchin Buckland, Priory and Preceptory, in the County of Somerset, by Thomas Hugo; Leopold Classic Library, 1861.

Hospitaller Women in the Middle Ages, edited by Anthony Luttrell and Helen J. Nicholson; Ashgate, 2006.

The Knights Hospitaller, by Helen J. Nicholson; Boydell Press, 2001.

Knight Hospitaller (1) 1100-1306 (Warrior Series), by David Nicolle and illustrated by Christa Hook; Osprey Publishing, 2001.

Knights of Jerusalem, the Crusading Order of Hospitallers 1100-1565, by David Nicolle; Osprey Publishing, 2008.

Hospitallers, the History of the Order of St. John, by Jonathan Riley-Smith; Hambledon Press, 1999.

The Knights Hospitaller in the Levant, c.1070-1309, by Jonathan Riley-Smith; Palgrave Macmillan, 2012.

Excavations at the Priory of the Order of the Hospital of St. John of Jerusalem, Clerkenwell, London, by Barney Sloane and Gordon Malcolm; Museum of London Archaeology Service, 2006.

A Cartulary of Buckland Priory in the County of Somerset, edited by the Rev. F. W. Weaver, M.A., F.S.A.; University of Michigan Libraries Collection, 1909.

To see more Poisoned Pen Press titles:

Visit our website: poisonedpenpress.com/
Request a digital catalog: info@poisonedpenpress.com